*Ladies and Gentlemen,
the Original Music
of the Hebrew Alphabet*

and

Weekend in Mustara

Other Novels by Curt Leviant

The Yemenite Girl

Passion in the Desert

The Man Who Thought He Was Messiah

Partita in Venice

Diary of an Adulterous Woman

*Ladies and Gentlemen,
the Original Music
of the Hebrew Alphabet*

and

Weekend in Mustara

Two Novellas

Curt Leviant

THE UNIVERSITY OF WISCONSIN PRESS

The University of Wisconsin Press
1930 Monroe Street
Madison, Wisconsin 53711

www.wisc.edu/wisconsinpress/
3 Henrietta Street
London WC2E 8LU, England

1   3   5   4   2

Printed in the United States of America

Library of Congress Cataloging-in-Publication Data
Leviant, Curt.
Ladies and gentlemen, the original music of the Hebrew alphabet, and,
Weekend in Mustara: two novellas / Curt Leviant.
pp.   cm.
ISBN 0-299-17950-8 (Cloth : alk. paper)
1. Manuscripts, Hebrew—Fiction.
2. Holocaust survivors—Fiction.
3. Budapest (Hungary)—Fiction.
4. Jews—Europe—Fiction.   5. Musicologists—Fiction.
6. Islands—Fiction.   7. Europe—Fiction.
I. Title: Ladies and gentlemen, the original music of the Hebrew alphabet,
and, Weekend in Mustara.   II. Leviant, Curt. Weekend in Mustara.
III. Title: Weekend in Mustara.   IV. Title.
PS3562.E8883 L48   2002
813'.54—dc21   2002003310

To

CHARLES FENYVESI
former editor of
The B'nai B'rith International Jewish Monthly

JOEL CARMICHAEL
former editor of *Midstream*

and

ROBERT MANDEL
who makes my literary dreams come true

Contents

Ladies and Gentlemen, the Original Music
    of the Hebrew Alphabet   3

Weekend in Mustara   81

*Ladies and Gentlemen,
the Original Music
of the Hebrew Alphabet*

I

"Doctor Gantz . . . Doctor Gantz," came the woman's voice from the doorway a moment after I'd left the restaurant. "You forgot your sweater."

Before I could turn back, the manager sent a little boy to bring it to me. From the top of the stone steps I looked down into the large sunny courtyard where groups of people stood scattered. Men came and went under the long stone archway that led to the street. Elderly women in kerchiefs sat on stone benches that faced the rear wall of the synagogue. Two lads in yarmulkes and payess stood talking, holding on to the wrought iron wedding canopy filigreed with Hebrew letters as though supporting it for some unseen couple. The shadows of the Hebrew words—bride and groom, I was told—were neatly imprinted on the stone floor. The sun still. The words did not move. Behind the concrete pillar at the foot of the steps a man waited. From where I stood only his head was visible, covered by the small black fedora that observant Jews wear the world over.

"Shalom. If I am not mistaken, you are from Israel," he said in heavily accented English, pounding in Hungarian fashion the first syllable of each word.

"No."

3

"Forgive me for intruding, but I heard you speaking with the rabbi in the dinning room, and I thought I heard some Hebrew words, so I assumed you lived there. Excuse me."

"It's okay. Don't worry about it."

"I am sorry to have taken the liberty."

"I assure you, no harm done." And then to make the man feel better, I added, "You speak an excellent English, sir."

He brightened. "But if you speak Hebrew, I can also converse with you in the holy tongue. Or others not so holy."

"I don't speak Hebrew . . . Have you ever been to Israel?" I asked just to be polite.

"Regretfully, I have never been to Israel, even though it is one of my fondest wishes to go."

Neither of us moved. I stood at the top of the steps, he behind the concrete pillar. I had the odd sensation I was speaking to a disembodied head. The man—he seemed to be about thirty or thirty-five, it was hard to tell—had high, wide cheekbones, a boyish face and large, bright, penetrating eyes. His full, luminous smile infused his entire face.

"Do you speak any other languages?"

"By all means. Yiddish, French, Hungarian of course, Russian, and Italian. Though I have never been to France, Russia, or Italy, though I have completed my studies in Frankfurt. And German, though my heart does not permit me to link it to—it is not worthy even of the category of *un*holy tongues. You understand?"

He made a little motion with his head to a bronze memorial tablet—engraved with a large *yorzeit* candle—on the courtyard wall.

I nodded. I knew what the Germans had done here.

4

"I have also never been to England or America, but I have traveled widely on the plains of Texas."

"Texas?" I asked incredulously.

"I have traveled widely in various places of the world—"

Only now, as I walked down the fifteen or twenty steps, did the rest of his body float into view.

"—without ever leaving the Budapest Library."

He was short, crippled in both legs, I saw; his hands were bent, but I noticed no sign of a hunched back or chest.

"You are from America, correct? I can tell by your accent. Are you . . ." he searched for a phrase—one of the few times I sensed him doing this—"having a good time?"

"Yes. Budapest is a beautiful city."

"Veneer," he said, still maintaining that broad childlike smile. He had the face of a boy, but as I drew closer I saw the slight lines on his forehead and on either side of his lips. "Pure veneer. But for a tourist, excellent. To understand, walk the darker streets, see the grey houses, do not go on the glittering boulevards, and you will see what I mean . . . You are a physician?"

"No."

"Because in the restaurant Madame Dalno—we call her the Czar," he whispered, "called you Doctor."

"I am a Ph.D."

"Oho, the gentleman possesses a doctorate. It is honor to make acquaintance of a fellow intellectual. In what speciality is your doctorate, may I ask?"

"Musicology. And yours?"

His mouth fell open. A red flush came over his cheeks, spread to his neck and temples. His eyes shone, on the verge of tears.

"I am very fortunate. I am so happy. Oh"—he clapped his hands together with a twist of one shoulder—"I do not know how to express myself. That I should have such good fortune, I did not know I am worthy of."

"Friedmann!" a voice shouted. We turned to the doorway. There stood Madame Dalno, hefty and double-chinned, with a round, humorless, officious face, hair wrapped in a white coif—she managed the Jewish community's combination free kosher kitchen and moderately priced restaurant.

"Friedmann! Please!" she shouted in English no doubt for my benefit. In courtly European fashion he tipped his hat to her. "Perhaps you are disturbing the Herr Doctor. Enough. He is a very busy man."

Friedmann withdrew. He gestured—was he teasing her?—the by-your-leave hand motion one sees in seventeenth-century French comedies. The color on his face subsided.

"A thousand pardons, Herr Doctor. I do not wish to rob the doctor of his precious time."

"Oh, no. No, no," I said. "A pleasure." I turned and said loudly to Madame Dalno: "Mister Friedmann honors me with his conversation." She closed the door.

Friedmann put his hand over his mouth and said softly, "The Czar is a very strong woman. Powerful is the word I mean to say. Like Biblical Joseph, provider of food."

As we spoke, several of the people in the courtyard drew near. One woman, with a sad face—wisps of black hair grew out of her chin and above her lip—tugged at my elbow. It dawned on me that one no longer saw such pathetic faces among older Jewish

6

women in New York. The face reminded me of pictures I'd seen of poor Jews in prewar Poland.

"Perhaps you can spare something for *tzedoke*," she said in Yiddish.

"Please," said a man with slightly crossed eyes. "I'm collecting for a poor family."

Others too stood with outstretched hands. I saw the tragic history of Hungarian Jewry etched into their faces. I reached into my pocket. How could my few forint help them?

A clap of hands. I turned to the doorway. Madame Dalno again, dispersing the beggars.

"When the Czar claps," Friedmann muttered, "people move. Meals without cost are not easy to come by."

"Mister Friedmann," I said.

"*Engineer* Friedmann," he said. "Ferdinand." He looked to the doorway before he spoke, then beckoned me away from the concrete pillar to the iron *chupa*. I walked in step with his halting stride.

"I cannot tell you how pleased I am that you are a musicologist, Herr Doctor."

"Please, my name is Isaac Gantz. I prefer not to be called Herr Doctor."

"If you please." He bowed his head. "At long last I have met someone in the field. And as a token of friendship I have something of interest which may excite curiosity."

"An old Hungarian folk instrument?"

"No. It has nothing to do with Hungary except that it has been here for a while. It concerns the alephbeys." Then, sensing a momentary hesitation in me, added, "The Hebrew alphabet."

"Well, Engineer Friedmann, I'm not really a linguist. It's music that interests me."

7

"I am not a linguist either, even though I speak seven languages. It is music that interests me as well. That is precisely, yes, yes," he cried in delight, "that is precisely what it is. Music. As da Vinci said: *'La figurazione delle cose invisibili'* . . . You look puzzled, Herr Doctor! Surely you know the great Leonardo's classic definition of music . . . the shaping of the invisible."

I nodded hesitantly. "A great genius, Leonardo."

"And a greater dilettante," Friedmann said. "He began a thousand projects, finished none. But his definition of music—oh, that is something. Pure music itself."

"Tell me, Engineer Friedmann, your alphabet, does it have neuma? Staves?"

"Pardon?"

"Excuse the terminology. It has notes?"

"Many things. Crucial. Old. Pristine. Seminal. It goes to the heart of the matter. To basics. To quote the old book of philosophy, it is so astounding that once you experience it, it is like the gallop of horses, horses of fire, horses of wrath, horses of darkness, horses of black night."

Friedmann looked at me as he recited with his clear blue eyes, eyes that held you, like hands firmly holding reins. "It tingles the sensations with horses of storm, horses of blood, horses of iron, horses of horror."

"The image alone gives me the creeps."

"Creeps? What is creeps?"

"Tingling of hair on back of my neck, shivers from galloping horses of horror and blood."

"A thousand pardons. I had no wish to frighten you. I merely wanted to give you feeling of what material I possess. You shall be delighted. Fascinated. This is my pledge."

"I'm fascinated already. Tell me what you're talking about."

"Of course. I have the knowledge of—that is to say, I am honored to be in possession of the original music of the Hebrew alphabet. With much supporting material."

"The what?"

"The original music of the Hebrew alphabet."

"I didn't even know there is such a thing."

"But there is. There is."

"Has it been published?"

"No, no. Not published."

"Not published? Incredible. Have you told anyone about this? Do they know?"

Friedmann put his hand over his mouth. "What do they know? What do they understand? If they see paper, they call it paper. Ink, they call it ink. But the mystery of ink on paper, quill on parchment, they do not understand. Some people, of course, I have told. Not major details. Not substance. Merely description. Outline. There is no one to talk to here."

"Well, you certainly can talk to me." I felt as though I'd stumbled onto the Rosetta Stone. A buzz of excitement crept along my skull, along the nape of my neck. In the nineteenth century, Mendelssohn discovered Bach. In the thirties, Bizet's Symphony in C was found. Not too long ago, a previously unknown Mendelssohn violin concerto was brought to light. Recently, someone found Max Bruch's Concerto for Two Pianos. It was always others, those fortunate others, who were graced with discovery. Perhaps now it was my turn. "If this is so, Engineer Friedmann, you may have one of the most valuable treasures in Jewish history, in the history of music. Possibly one of the most astounding finds in the history of world culture."

Friedmann lowered his eyes. "I am a modest man."

"Where is this item? How did you find it?"

"How did I find it? It is a long story, Doctor Isaac. Now is not the time. What are you doing in Budapest, may I ask?"

"I was at the International Congress of Musicology in Vienna, and since Budapest is so close, I decided to visit. May I see your item? Perhaps we'll photograph it and publish the document. Maybe I can publicize it for you in the musical world."

"Everything is possible. If—" Friedmann stopped.

"If what?"

"If you fulfill my request."

"Sure. What is it?"

"You probably live in New York. Oh, how foolish of me! Of *course* you do. All Jews live in New York!"

"Not all, but many. What can I do for you?"

"Please find my relatives."

At that moment I felt I stood in a fairy-tale world. The king shows me his daughter. I fall madly in love with her. Then the wizard imposes on me an impossible task: to win the princess' hand. I had already seen myself and my find pictured on page one of the *New York Times,* with the headline:

MUSICOLOGIST REPORTS MAJOR DISCOVERY:
ORIGINAL MUSIC OF HEBREW ALPHABET

"Where should I look for your relatives?"

"In America. That is, New York."

"I'll do my best. But what has that to do with scholarly material? With our research?"

"It has everything to do with it. My relatives are important for me."

"I promise I shall do my best as soon as I return to the United States," I said, rather insulted. "Can you imagine a man not keeping a promise to help find relatives? I consider this a sacred mission. Why are you smiling, Engineer Friedmann?"

Friedmann tilted his head, looked up at me. There was just a hint of a laugh at the edges of his almond-shaped eyes, deep-set like the eyes of Polish Jews.

"Because I have sad experience. If you will be so kind as to excuse me, but I cannot help smiling to myself at this protestation. I see many Jews here over the months. Of course I cannot talk to all. But I search out a sympathetic face—I usually stand by that pillar at the foot of the steps—and analyze to myself if that person can be approached. All are friendly. As anyone who takes the interest to visit the Jewish restaurant and communal offices of the *kehilla* must be. But somehow something always happens to this good intentionness by time they return to America. Many promised, none kept."

"No problem, I'm sure. All I have to do is get hold of a Manhattan phone book."

"But they live in New York."

"Manhattan is New York, and in a few minutes I can find out if they are there."

"It is very kind of you. You understand my point of view."

"Of course. But, frankly, I'm disappointed. You sparked my interest. I don't know if I can come back again. Travel is expensive, and every year the dollar gets devaluated. I'm only a teacher in a small college." I bent close to him and said softly, "I'll tell you confidentially, I must publish an important study in order to retain my job."

"You mean that in America, in free America, they will discharge you from your post if you do not publish something in a journal or in a book?"

"The system is called publish or perish."

"Oh, that is terrible. Ay, ay! In free America." He shook his head. "In the great land! Here under the Germans the system was called Hungarian or perish. If you were not a Hungarian, meaning that you were a Jew, you were shot by the river, not more that a five-minute tram ride from here. Later they refined it to the death camps."

"You are mistaken, Engineer Friedmann."

"I am not. Not. Not." He bounced awkwardly on his toes, one bent foot rising before the other. "I lived through it. I saw my parents, my sisters, my friends slain. In this city of beautiful buildings, beautiful veneer. Only I survived. The last of the noble family of Friedmanns. That I do not want to hear. From an American who was not here."

"A thousand pardons, Engineer Friedmann." I put my hand on my heart. "I don't want to see you angry. Of course I don't doubt your word, I know what happened here, but it's about publish or perish that you're mistaken. It's not capital punishment, God forbid, but perish in the sense that you lose your job. Jobs are scarce now. People with Ph.D.s are driving taxis, serving as waiters, working in the post office. One doesn't know whether to call one's mailman mister or doctor. I can't see myself in the post office; I'd rather die."

Friedmann put out his hands, palms up. Two fingers of his left hand were gnarled, the joints protruding. "Please. Life is foremost. That is my entire philosophy. No dying." He clapped his hands over his ears. His elbows jutted out at odd angles. "That I refuse to hear."

"Because when I was in college, I worked ten nights at the post office, while I went to school during the day. Sheer torture. Never again. Even if you don't show me the manuscript, at least describe its contents. If you do me that favor or give me sufficient background, I'll be able to write . . ."

"No, no. No writing. This belongs to me. Us."

"Us?"

"Us!" Friedmann asserted.

"Us—you and me?" I asked.

"Us, yes. But not you and me. Us is my colleague and me. My partner. Ferenc Fürer."

"You didn't tell me there are two people in this."

"My dear Doctor. There are many things I did not tell you. One cannot work alone. You said writing. Absolutely not. I refuse." He clapped his crooked hands over his ears again. Smiled a wry smile. "I won't hear of it."

I drew a deep breath. "You don't understand. I won't publish it. But on an application for a scholarship, stipendium, to pay for my travel expenses, if I give an indication of its contents, I may be able to get money to return here to study further . . . Otherwise I won't be able to come back . . . with your relatives' addresses."

"You will. Don't worry, you will."

"So I may come talk to you?"

Friedmann shifted weight on his legs. Evidently it was hard for him to remain in one position for any length of time. Perhaps it was hard for him to be on his feet altogether, and here I was standing with him for more than half an hour, without even making an offer to sit down on a park bench or at a café.

He smiled. "I agree, but you must understand the compact we made. You provide addresses of my

relatives—by mail—and then we get deeper into
material."

Friedmann stretched out his hand. I shook it. I expected it to be moist, nervous; but it was warm and dry,
surprisingly soft, hairless, babyish. He had thin wrists.
A child's hand.

"When will you come?" he asked.

"Is tomorrow after lunch good for you?"

"Why not?" He hitched up one shoulder and with
an awkward but evidently practiced movement went
into his pocket and pressed into my hand a soft off-
white card that had been in his wallet for years.

"My visit card. Note the address. Not too distant
from this point. Excuse fourth floor . . . Now if you
will be so kind, take out pen and write down names of
people you will find for me."

He dictated and I jotted down names, relationships,
places of birth, and occupations. Then he said,
"Adieu," turned swiftly and hobbled away.

II

I walk around Budapest, the city of someone else's dreams. Marvel at the architecture, the grace of the skyline, the seven bridges, each with a history of its own. I peel veneer, replace veneer. I cross and recross the Chain Bridge that spans the calm Blue Danube so often I feel it's mine. But dare not look down at the water for fear I may see red. I love the silhouette of the elegant grey buildings along the river, so old-world European.

I walk to Friedmann's house. Here at this busy corner, where my hotel is located, under the colonnade, at the entrance to the new subway with its high-speed escalators, at the corner of the modern American-style supermarket where some red godling has spilled his cornucopia into baskets and aisles, at this juncture of satiety—here I see a seventeen-year-old newsboy selling a paper for half a forint: how much profit can the poor guy make? I buy a paper even though I don't read Hungarian: by the third day he knows me and smiles hello—here the Ghetto wall was erected; here Hungarians who had been neighbors with Jews for decades turned them over to the Germans when they made their roundups; here Mrs. Basanyi said sweetly, "Herr Offizer, Mrs. Schneider is still upstairs with a sprained ankle," and then the Germans and their Hungarian helpers took all the Jews of the courtyard, including Mrs. Schneider, took all the Jews of all the courtyards, and shot them by the river, at the foot of the iron Chain Bridge.

Then I came to Friedmann's apartment, two poorly illuminated rooms on the fourth floor of a walkup. He must have had iron will, and iron strength, to drag himself down and up once, perhaps twice, a day. I knocked on the open door and, hearing no reply, entered. The small kitchen had a bare wooden table, one chair, an electric hot plate, and a small cabinet on the wall above the tiny, single-faucet sink. The streaked white walls hadn't been painted in years. Cartons and paper-wrapped packages tied with string were scattered on the floor, as though Friedmann had just moved in, or was preparing to move out.

Friedmann entered from another room, formally attired in fedora, Sabbath jacket, tie, and ill-matching trousers. A wave of pity came over me. He stood there, as if saying: This is what I possess. I wanted to forget the material which would serve only me, and just ask Friedmann all about himself. Where he came from, where he'd been born, where educated, who supported him. I wanted to know who were his kin, why he didn't work at his profession, what happened to him during the war. Was his infirmity from birth, or had the Germans tortured and crippled him; or, no less cruel, in fact more eager, the Hungarians?

"You have captured my attention," Friedmann began and thrust aside my thoughts. "And if I may say so, my dear Herr Doctor, my affection as well."

He pulled out the chair and asked me to sit.

"No, thank you, Engineer Friedmann, you sit please. I can stand."

"Oh no. You are my guest. I insist, you please. Sit down."

"No. I shall not do it."

"Then neither shall I," he said, smiling stubbornly. We both stood. He leaned on the chair.

"You have done me a great kindness in coming to visit me."

"Actually, Engineer Friedmann, yours is the kindness."

"No, it is a great honor for me." He smiled again, his smooth face radiant and luminous. A question teased me. I didn't want to ask if he'd been born infirm. If Friedmann wanted to tell me, I would gladly listen; but I would not be the first to ask. As he spoke, his eyes darted, danced, sparkled like a child's, seeing more than they saw. "Although I do not have too many visitors here in my humble abode, I welcome each one to the best of my ability. If I have not apologized for it yet, I hope you will excuse my small English. I have not spoken so much English since my schooling. I hope I do not intrude upon, or offend, your developed sensibilities of style."

"On the contrary, Engineer Friedmann," I said, falling willy-nilly into that bookish English he occasionally used. "I hasten to assure you of my complete and thoroughgoing respect and admiration for your mastery of the English tongue."

Friedmann bowed his head. "I am grateful to you, and although I am still abiding by our agreement of yesterday, which agreement we have sealed with the indelible bonds of a handshake—a form of swearing, not

17

so, Herr Doctor?—and hence shall not at this time reveal any more about our common matter of interest; nevertheless, to show you how much I am interested in your welfare, I shall read you a sort of prolegomenon. Please concentrate."

He cleared his throat, took a folded page from his jacket pocket; and with one hand behind his back, and one leg thrust slightly forward, he began to read, even chant, with the rocking motion of a man davenning in shul.

"The secret of the aleph-beys was handed over personally by the Angel Raziel to Adam who gave it to Abel. His brother Cain was jealous and killed him for it. It was then taken from Cain. As soon as the mark was placed on his forehead Cain forgot the melody, which was held for some ten generations until it was given to Noah after the Flood, and then to the Patriarch Abraham, whose Hebrew name I have the honor of bearing. His son Ishmael was caught stealing the alphabet by Sarah, and for this Sarah drove Ishmael and his mother Hagar from the house. Abraham gave the music of the alphabet to Isaac, and Isaac intended to give it to Esau, in payment for the prepared meals that his hunter son served him. However, in a dream, an angel—I do not know if it was Raziel or not—told him to give it to Jacob. In a historic encounter, Jacob later wrestled with the angel Raziel who tried, a test it was, to take back the secret music of the alphabet, but Jacob prevailed. He had passed the test of strength and only suffered a wound in his thigh bone, which made him limp. Jacob, in turn, passed the music on to Joseph, who earned the enmity of his brothers, for Joseph, to tease his brothers, foolishly chanted parts of the alphabet but never sang a complete letter to them.

"And so it went from generation to generation. David was inspired by the melodies to compose the Psalms. He too teased with the melody, playing—like Joseph—parts of it for Saul. This drove Saul to the verge of madness and once in frustration he even threw a spear at David. Fortunately, it missed.

"So much for people. Now to the Hebrew alphabet itself. In the aleph-beys there are twenty-two letters, a fact attested to by philologists and even the medieval kabbalists and philosophers who were experts at using the aleph-beys for their own purposes."

Here Friedmann lowered his script and added: "I just mention this to let you know that twenty-two is not an artificial designation, twisted out of context just to make it fitting my theory. I am not like the arrogant nineteenth-century German Bible critics who pro-pounded a theory and then chopped and edited Holy Scripture to make it fit their preconceived hypothesa. If we write out the basic letters of the aleph-beys, or as the Sefardim say it, aleph-bet, we will note, then, twenty-two letters."

Friedmann drew a deep breath, almost a sigh, and continued reading:

"In our musical system of notation there are twelve notes. On the piano, seven white keys, five black. On the violin, no colors. In the Hebraic system of conver-gences and correspondences, there is balance, evenness, parallelism—the hallmark of Biblical poetry. And there are the ten sefirot, the fiery numbered characteristics of God, which as the Zohar, the classic text of Jewish mys-ticism, teaches us are the foundation of the entire work of creation. The twelve notes which are heard but not seen, and the ten sefirot which are neither heard nor seen, but are of a sublime musical fire, make up the number twenty-two, which corresponds meticulously to the sum of Hebrew letters, and just as in Kabbala where there is union of heavenly and earthly, and each chooses his partner in fusion, so the twenty-two letters wed the note-sefirot combination of twenty-two. Of the twenty-two letters, ten are imperfect because they are, or can be, finalized, or can change their sound and shape according to position and grammatical rules. Twelve are absolutes, firm, immutable in sound. To these twelve the twelve notes go; the weaker ten need the divine fire, the heavenly music of the sefirot in order to become whole . . . Do you follow?"

"Yes," I said politely. My head was reeling. Against my will Friedmann's words had seduced me, attracted me into listening, unable to respond or frame rebuttal. "I am trying to follow. This is all new to me. May I take notes?"

"Notes? You must be jesting. I have no notes to give you now. I am not going to—I have no intention of singing the alphabet—"

"No, no," I laughed at the pun I had inadvertently created. "Not musical notes. I meant notations. Note-taking, as in notebook."

"No, no. No note-taking. Please do not take my notes. What I am saying you must remember. It is very complex. It will get more complex, but you must be worthy, note-worthy," he laughed, his body shaking. "Yes, you may consider this a test. Consider yourself fortunate."

"I do. I do," I said, and did not know if I was mocking myself, or him—my dream wizard made manifest—in my loud assertation.

"There are so many convergences and correspondences here—I shall get to them in a moment—that you will jump with delight at the perfection of the blending of all three items, yes, their uncanny musical genius, their divine order, for it is nothing if not divine."

I felt uncomfortable, for the introduction of the divine into what was, or appeared to be, a scientific, scholarly matter made me suspect that it might not be fully reliable. Yet Friedmann's words fascinated me. Owing to my limited Jewish knowledge, I did not understand the esoteric part too well, but I certainly wanted to hear more. Friedmann did not change his position, but read as though delivering a formal lecture in an academic setting. Since he paused, I asked:

"Do you play any instrument?" And only after I had uttered the words did I realize the insensitivity, the stupidity of my question. As soon as I said it, I saw those malformed bones and awry hands pressing my retina with guilt.

"No," he said slowly, "but perhaps yes. I sing. My voice is my instrument. I have been told I have an excellent voice. When I have been a boy I sang in the shul choir. During my *Ovinu malkenu* solo the women's section was flooded with tears."

I looked around for Friedmann's books. Perhaps he kept them in his little bedroom or in the cabinet on the wall.

"Where are your books?"

"I have no books. I have marvels far greater than books."

"No books? An intellectual like you? Not even one?"

He shook his head. "Not one. The prayers and the Bible I know by heart."

"Would you like some? I'll be glad to give you any books you request."

"Not needed. What need have I of books? I have too many possessions as is. My collection of books, one of the finest in the world, is in the library. It teaches me many things. For instance, I have never been to Tibet, but I know more about that land than the Dalai Lama himself."

"Are you finished with your presentation?"

"Finished? Hardly have I begun." Then he held his head. "Oh, I am so apologetic. Here you are standing and I have not even offered you anything. May I offer you a cup of tea?"

"No, thank you. I've just eaten."

"It is just as well. I have no sugar and I am out of tea."

"Well, I could say, like the lady in the comedy: boil me a cup of water."

"That is amusing, but my electric ring is broken too."

Not knowing what else to say, I commiserated, "I'm sorry to hear that."

We stood there in silence looking at each other.

Finally Friedmann, shaking his head, said, "That is all for today."

"But what about the melody? The original music of the Hebrew alphabet," I raised my voice against my will. "Can't you give me a hint? Like Joseph did his brothers? Or David to Saul?"

"Oh," he said, smiling coyly, his face luminescent as an angel's. "I do not like to tease people. Remember our agreement, our oath? . . . But let me assure you that you will return, and that you will get a stipendium."

"How do you know?"

"I know. I know many people who come here. Important people. You will be back."

As I left him, Friedmann replaced his manuscript in his jacket pocket and with much difficulty began unknotting his tie.

III

A few minutes after I'd cleared customs at Kennedy I ran to the nearest phone booth, pulled out my passport folder, and looked for Friedmann's list. A sour feeling—lost, all is lost—went through me, as I emptied the folder, searched my pockets. I couldn't find the card on which I'd written the addresses. At home I made a thorough search of my luggage. Zero. I knew I'd put Friedmann's address list in a safe place, among my important papers. Then I remembered: his visiting card. But I couldn't find that either. At first I didn't panic, for I knew that if I didn't find it here, I'd find it there. In a pocket of a suitcase, in a fold of a briefcase. Again a thorough search was in vain. I had misplaced both the names of the lost and the name of the seeker. Now I couldn't even—assuming that I'd irretrievably lost the visiting card—write to Friedmann (an embarrassment I was prepared to undergo) to provide me with a list of his relatives again. Could it be that I'd purposely—subconsciously—misplaced the card, not to avoid looking for his relatives—an oath, a handshake I considered sacred—but perhaps because deep down I wanted to have no part of the original music of the Hebrew alphabet, for I suspected its authenticity? Again and again I searched the contents of my billfold—sentimental, I keep calling cards, scraps of notes, hotel bills, train tickets—they provide me with the aura of travel when I'm immobile. I went through all my shirts, jackets, trousers—once I felt something in a jacket pocket—an old photograph of myself: my image mocking me. I searched the manuscripts and books I'd taken along, in the hope that I'd left the list as a bookmark or inadvertently placed it among other papers. Nothing. I remembered only Friedmann's name and the floor he lived on. In Budapest, I'd find him. But returning to Budapest without finding his relatives was senseless. It was painful to imagine Friedmann laughing at me as yet another in the long line of friendly but unreliable American tourists.

That piece of paper haunted me. I hate to lose things; rarely misplace anything. Once more I went through my billfold, my folders. In vain. A sense of emptiness gnawed at me.

Then I had an idea. I don't know why I hadn't thought of it before. In the library I found a Jewish yearbook, and looked up the addresses of the Budapest Jewish communal offices. Then I wrote four letters: to Madame Dalno, to Friedmann c/o Madame Dalno, to the rabbi I'd met in the dining room, and to a prominent scholar and communal leader, Doctor Laszlo Geller.

Two months passed without a reply. Perhaps, I thought, I could find a Hungarian Jew going to visit Budapest who would reestablish my links with Friedmann. The unfulfilled promise made me miserable: It hung like a weight on my skull. Meanwhile, things were getting worse at the college. Directives came down that faculty was to be cut, and that even sacrosanct tenure, which I had hoped to get some day, was to be abolished. As a junior member of the faculty, with relatively few publications and a specialty that wasn't really marketable, I was particularly vulnerable. The original music of the Hebrew alphabet was tantalizingly further out of reach.

Then one day, with a suddenness that still surprises me, I opened my passport folder, pulled out some scraps of paper searching for a hotel bill for income tax purposes, and came upon Friedmann's list. I danced around the room with joy. How had I found it? It had been there all along. On the reverse side of a card filled with names of contacts in Vienna; *that's* the side I'd always looked at. I simply had not bothered to turn the card over. And there too I had also copied Friedmann's address.

Coincidentally—of course, Friedmann would contend kabbalistic convergence—that same day a reply came from Doctor Geller, director of the Budapest Jewish Historical Institute, with Friedmann's address and a brief postscript: "Why do you want it?" In a note of thanks for his courtesy I told Geller briefly: my interest in research in old music.

Next I got hold of the Manhattan phone book and looked for an Albert Bok. Of the three Boks listed one was Hung Pheng Bok, hardly a middle European; another was John Bok, rejected as out of clan; the third was Sarah Bok.

She answered on the second ring. Her Viennese-accented English indicated I was on the right track.

"Hello, my name is Doctor Gantz. I met an Engineer Ferdinand Friedmann in Budapest and he asked me to try to locate some relatives named Bok. Are you by any chance related to an Ignatz Friedmann who owned a chocolate factory in Vienna before the Second World War?"

"Yes," she said happily. "Ignatz was not *my* uncle, but the relative of my late husband, Albert. His mother was a Friedmann."

We chatted a few minutes and then she gave me the number of her husband's cousin, Wolfgang Leopold Bok, in Atlantic City, New Jersey. I warmed to the name, assuming that the man might be interested in music, but he turned out to be a merchant.

I dialed, and a cultivated European voice answered.

"Hello, this is Doctor Gantz. I have regards from a long-lost relative of yours in Budapest, Engineer Ferdinand Friedmann." I recounted my meeting with him and his desire to find members of his family, and then read the entire list of relatives, where they'd lived, what they'd done. And then I gave him Friedmann's address. Bok recognized all the names, except Ferdinand Friedmann's.

"I'll tell you the truth, Doctor. Him I haven't heard of. But I thank you for bringing this to my attention. I'll call my relatives tonight."

"And I'll write Friedmann tonight that I found you. I consider this miraculous. One opens up a phone book and there, because of the right combinations, fortuitous circumstances, one finds relatives for a man thousands of miles away."

I could have sworn I was happier than he.

I sent my letter to Friedmann registered, return receipt requested. A month went by, two months. I called Bok and he told me rather curtly that he'd written but received no reply. If Ferdinand Friedmann were *really* interested in his new-found relative—Bok's tone had a more than vaguely accusatory tone directed towards

me—he'd have written by now. I sensed Bok repri-
manding me for having instigated this relative hunt, as
if I were at fault both for having brought up the Friedmann affair, *and* for Friedmann not responding. To
impress Bok, I kept accenting phrases such as, "So
Friedmann said to me 'Doctor Gantz, I'd be so happy if
you could find my relatives,'" and "in my capacity as an
objective person, a doctor, I find that . . ." which was a
radical departure for a man like me who insisted on
being called Mister, not Doctor.

"Well, why didn't he answer me?" Bok insisted.

"He might not have answered," I said lamely, "because he is sick, or perhaps because he didn't get the letter. Did you send it registered?"

"No."

"I sent mine registered. With return receipt."

"Who signed it? Friedmann?"

"No. That is sort of strange, isn't it? The receipt
came back, but not with his signature. Perhaps the jan-
itor took the letter and signed for it—and perhaps he
brought it to the fourth floor, perhaps not. After all,
Hungary is a communist land, a dictatorship. Perhaps
whoever signed for it never gave him the letter."

"Well," Bok said, "the whole thing is puzzling. Neither I nor my wife remember him."

"Yet Friedmann seems to know not only everyone
in the family, but their occupations and businesses as
well, and the fact that they're in America. Maybe—"

But I stopped. I didn't say: Maybe he's being rejected because he's a cripple and nobody wants to have
anything to do with him.

"Maybe what?"

"Maybe you'll still hear from him."

"Could be. Thank you."

And I replied: "I'm glad to do my part. As a physician, one has duties and obligations that go beyond the Hippocratic Oath."

Several more weeks passed. In the spring I was worrying if my annual contract would be renewed, and if I'd get a travel grant to Budapest to further my research. Friedmann's silence disappointed me. It baffled and angered me as well. I kept my word; why didn't he have the courtesy to respond? But even after I'd put him out of mind, his manuscript kept surfacing. I didn't want to discuss the find with professionals, lest my territorial rights be violated, and lest—let me be frank—they laugh at me. Nevertheless, I checked into articles, listings, encyclopedias, at various Jewish, public, and university libraries. I went through the *Index of Jewish Indexes,* the *Index of Jewish Periodicals,* the *Index of Jewish Festschrifts,* and the *Bibliography of Jewish Bibliographies,* but found nothing that remotely resembled Friedmann's subject.

Then I received two letters. The first came from Friedmann.

Dear Doctor Gantz:
   I am glad I have the honoured opportunity of writing in response to your kind letter. You are very gracious. You made a promise, and kept your promise, for the delayed fulfillment of which I am certain you had ample reasons. I admire your kept promise. It is an honour to write to you, a Professor of your high Reputation.
   First, I want to apologize heartily at why I have not replied to your kind letter, and for your kind deed of providing my relatives' addresses. The

reason was not neglect, nor ingratitude, God forbid. It is because I was at hospital briefly, but thank God, I am much better now. I am sorry if I have given you worrisomeness. I am flattered that a person of your ~~elevation~~ elevated distinction is interested in me, in my life and in my work.

If I may be permitted to coin a phrase, or a word, in a language that is native to you, but for me only an acquired experience, something studied in my youth, spoken some, but written not too often, for which to my regrets I have little occasion to put into practise due to the small use of English in my circle, and also regrettably to the general lack of cultured people here—I do not wish to wrong them, God forbid, by implying that they are not cultured—Jews and lack of culture is an anomaly; yet as cultured as they are in Judacia in their own limited way, in the religious aspects of Jewishness, and in Hebrew, they know none of English or of secular culture, music, theater, they close their minds to it, poor souls, and even look at it with suspicion, as if one cannot serve God with all one's might and soul, and still have knowledge of secular arts; hence there is small opportunity for me to practise this noble tongue, and this is another reason I stand where I met you on that fortuitous occasion and look for someone intelligent to whom I can speak in English or Hebrew, or any other foreign tongue.

What I wanted to say, and having begged your leave to indulge in a neologism, I sought to tell you a little something of my past, that I have always been a breadloser in my family, owing to my condition, and to my predilection for thought and ideas rather than the more ignoble side of life. I will perhaps explain this jocular turn of phrase in a later letter, or if God willing, we meet again in Budapest, as I have every hope that you will come back, for if you recall when you expressed your doubts as to your financial ability to return I said to you: "You will. Don't worry, you will."

I am honoured to engage in a correspondence with you, esteemed Herr Doctor, and only wish to inform you as of now that I was born in Budapest, and received my engineering education in Frankfurt, upon the completion of which I returned to Budapest where I have remained ever since, sharing the same fate of my fellow Jews during the bestial German occupation, and three months in Auschwitz, but miraculously surviving. While writing to you, I have at this same time written to my relatives in New Jersey. Once again, I beg you to accept my gratitude for your kindness in helping me to locate members of my dear family.

Sincerely yours,
Ferdinand Friedmann, B.Sc.Eng.

But of the manuscript, not a word.

The second letter was from Professor Geller. In my excitement, I skimmed it first, catching snatches of phrases: "scholarly," brilliant," "the music of the alphabet," "intriguing," "moonlight." But as I carefully re-read the letter, written in elegant English, I got a different message.

Dear Doctor Gantz

I am glad that you took the trouble to reply to my query as to why you want Friedmann's address, and I hope that my inquisitiveness will not be a disservice to you.

Please be informed that Friedmann, God save us, is an unfortunate man who cannot be depended upon to consistently behave in a rational manner. The original music of the Hebrew alphabet has been his idée fixe, his joint enterprise with a friend of his, his partner and driving force, who unfortunately must also be placed in the same mental category. If you wish, I can offer some examples of the far-fetched projects they have pitifully attempted to propound:

1) Saving coffee grounds to do research on their possible conversion to practical use.
2) Printing money on vitamin-enriched edible paper, so that if there is not enough food to purchase for the money, one could as a last resort, eat the money for food.
3) Harnessing the energy of moonlight.

The above absurd ideas are regularly presented as "scholarly papers" by the team of Fürer and Friedmann, the two madmen of Budapest. But there is nothing more otherworldly and insane (perhaps even brilliantly insane) than this original music of the Hebrew alphabet. I urge you not to involve yourself; and should you be thinking of this in scholarly terms, as a possibly intriguing element of a long-lost world, do not delude yourself with false hopes any longer, lest later disappointment be more severe than earlier.

Sincerely yours,
Dr. Laszlo Geller
P.S. I trust I shall have the opportunity of
making your acquaintance should you be in
Budapest again.

My first reaction to the letter was disbelief. One
cannot dismiss a man as a madman just because he has
something astounding to offer the world. I mulled over
Doctor Geller's letter for a week; meanwhile, I had occasion to read some articles and a news item in the Saturday *New York Times* patents column that gave me
some satisfaction.

Dear Dr. Geller:
Many thanks for your cordial letter. I appreciate
your kindness in trying to do me a good turn, but
I do not think that at this stage I should reject out
of hand Friedmann's discovery. I have heard him
read to me salient parts of his "paper," as you call
it, and I was impressed by his articulation. I would
respectfully add that in the history of culture, new
discoveries and inventions have always been
labeled the products of madmen. To support the
above contention I am enclosing a Xerox copy of
an article in last Saturday's *New York Times* which
lists as a new patent by a team of industrial
scientists from the Nescafe corporation, an
innovative method for inexpensively converting
coffee grounds into useable paper. This is just one
example of showing how rather than being a
madman, Friedmann has elements of genius. Is it
possible that you may have misjudged him?

I shall be honored to make your acquaintance if
I am in Budapest, this summer, as I hope to be.
Sincerely,
Isaac Gantz, Ph.D.
Instructor of Musicology
Frederick Cole College

Then I called Bok.

"Ah yes, Doctor, thanks for calling. I did hear from
Engineer Friedmann only recently—"

"I thought you would, Mister Bok. For I got a letter
from him stating that he'd written to you."

"But I confess that the story is not much clearer. As
I told you, we do not recall any Ferdinand Friedmann.
I still don't know Ferdinand's father's name. And there
is another puzzle here. Our family was in Vienna from
1929 to 1938. Friedmann knew we lived there; it is obvious from all the notes. Why did he not attempt to contact us then?"

"I don't know. Perhaps I'll write to him," I said.

"What does he want?" Bok said impatiently. "And
why did he wait so long before answering?"

I imagined Bok as an intelligent man in his fifties,
barrel-chested, muscular, hairy, of middle height. A
man whose broad face flushed—as it no doubt did
now—when he was upset or angry.

"He was hospitalized," I said. "He explained that in
his letter to me."

"What puzzles us is: why did this sudden interest
flourish now?"

"Perhaps he lost contact," I suggested.

"Tell me. Does he want any material help? He
doesn't mention it in his letter."

"He specifically told me he doesn't want money. He is just yearning for some contact. He begged me: 'Doctor Gantz, I would like to find my relatives.' I think, Mr. Bok, you should realize how hard it is for them in Europe, especially Hungary. They have no means of getting—"

I myself don't know how I finished the sentence. I felt that Bok suspected me of creating a relative; that I was involved in some sort of con game. I suppose it *was* odd. What if some stranger had called *me* up and told *me* he'd met a relative of mine I'd never heard of in some godforsaken land? Wouldn't *I* be wary? Wouldn't I think that I might be a victim of some con game which would sooner or later cost me money? But, curiously, the suspicion I sensed in his hesitant voice prompted the same in me—a sort of sympathetic vibration, fanned in part by Professor Geller's letter, a letter whose contents I'd rejected.

"Just a second. Someone's at the door. Call you back in a minute." I hung up and walked around the room. Perhaps during the war Friedmann had met a man with a name like his—to be drawn to someone with a like name is perfectly natural, especially during wartime, and especially if someone is crippled and completely alone—and from him he learned the history of the Friedmann family, and the names of relatives which he remembered. And so Ferdinand Friedmann, lonely, forlorn, poor, ill, unfamilied, an orphan in every sense of the word, Ferdinand had in all innocence—I hesitate to think it was cunning or malice; those terms would be obscene in reference to Friedmann—arrogated the other Friedmann's family as his own, and even after separation, or perhaps after the other's death, considered himself the rightful heir to this family list, and made plans to contact members of his family, perhaps even as a memorial to the deceased Friedmann, a way of resurrecting him. But why Ferdinand had waited so long was as much of a puzzle to me as it was to Bok.

Then I dialed Bok's number again. "Hello. I'm back," and told him—knowing that I was drawing myself deeper into the suspected con game by speaking of money—that Ferdinand lived in very poor circumstances, and that he was deserving of help, that indeed I had already helped him out with a gift of cash.

"Now, well, that I didn't know. He said nothing about that in his letter."

"I'm sure he wouldn't. He doesn't *want* his newfound relationship with you to be built on a donor-taker basis."

"I appreciate that," Bok said.

"So I suggest you don't offer anything to him the first time you write, so it doesn't break the web for him, so to speak. By the third exchange of letters you might do it discreetly. I leave it to you. As a European who knows the propensity of American relatives disappearing with the very first hint of a request for aid, he is surely avoiding it. Friedmann, however, repeated to me that he wants no money. Just contact with relatives."

I hesitated again, and then said what in retrospect I should not have said, for by saying it I may have spoiled Friedmann's chances of coming to the United States—for perhaps *that* had been his intent all along. In fact, while thinking that I recalled an aside of his, sent across the back of his hand, with an exaggerated stage whisper, right after Madame Dalno had been waved away:

"Please don't tell anyone, Doctor, but I have had the honor of being invited to serve as engineer in America. I don't know yet if I will go, but I'm not telling anyone here"—and his large blue eyes shifted back and forth—"because of possible jealousy. They are very jealous when someone gets a chance to leave for America."

This I dismissed as a fantasy when I heard it. Simply put, I didn't believe Friedmann. Not the way he looked. However, it was his only statement that I didn't take at face value. I didn't blend this disbelief to any of his other remarks. So when I told Bok that Ferdinand Friedmann was also a cripple, it was too late to withdraw, even though Bok didn't hear me too well, for he asked me to repeat what I'd said. What else could I have substituted, even if I'd had the presence of mind to change the word at the last moment? Pimple? Your cousin has a pimple. Nipple? Pickle?

"A cripple," I said. "He is a short, deformed man, whose legs are lame and whose hands are bent. And with these legs the poor man must climb four flights to his tiny apartment."

"Oh," Bok said. "That I didn't know either. He didn't mention that aspect of himself either."

I bit my tongue. Too late. I had just destroyed my friend as a normal human being in the eyes of his unseen relatives, and reduced him to an object of pity.

"I didn't think Friedmann would. He doesn't want anyone to feel sorry for him."

"And you didn't mention it when you called the first time."

"Didn't I?"

"No, you didn't, Doctor."

"I thought I mentioned it in passing."

"No. I would have remembered that. In any case, thank you very much for your interest. You have admirable concern for another human being."

"Thank you," I said, wondering if Bok, in his subtle European way, was slyly baiting me. "But despite his deformity he's a brilliant man, with the sort of syncretic intellect one associates with the finest European minds."

"May I ask you, Doctor, what you were doing in Budapest? It's not exactly the playground of Europe."

"Well, part vacation, curiosity, a search."

"Search?"

"For research."

"Of course, you are a doctor. What is your medical specialty?"

Now he had me. I had set the pattern with my little misleading use of title in order to gain greater credence for myself. I was afraid that if I told him I was in the field of music he might view me as a long-haired, depraved drummer, always on a high, an irresponsible *artiste* who could not be trusted.

"Medieval and Renaissance music."

"For curative purposes?"

"Pardon?"

"I say, you utilize this for curative purposes, Doctor, perhaps for the mentally disturbed?"

"Oh, you misunderstand. I'm not a *doctor* doctor."

"But I asked what your medical specialty was and you said medieval music."

"I'm sorry, I misheard you. I have a doctorate in music."

"I could have sworn," Bok said, "that you told me that as a physician you have duties that go beyond the call of the Hippocratic Oath."

"I said, as a musician, not physician, and I was using Hippocratic Oath only metaphorically."

"Then I must have misheard. I was under the distinct impression with your repeated use of doctor that you were a physician."

"Musician."

"You play an instrument?"

"Oh no," I said. "I'm not an instrumentalist."

"You sound so indignant."

"Well, I do research in musicology. I'm not a mere performer." There was no need telling a complete stranger about the embattled division in the field of music between those who only played, and those who thought, analyzed, discovered, described, made sense and order out of the chaos of the creative tradition.

I sensed that since he'd discovered I wasn't a physician the scale tipped; I no longer had the upper hand.

"Tell me, how does this Friedmann interest you?"

"Like any other human being would interest me," I said somewhat aggressively. "In any part of the world, especially behind the Iron Curtain, which place I doubt you've been, if a Jew comes up to me with tears in his eyes and presses a list of names into my hand and pleads, 'Find my relatives,' wouldn't you consider this a sacred obligation, a mitzva of the highest order?"

"I would, Doctor. You are perfectly right."

"Excuse me," I lied, "my doorbell is ringing again. Good talking to you."

"Goodbye, Doctor, and thank you. We'll be in touch."

"I hope so. I've grown fond of your cousin."

"Perhaps in due time we can solve the family mystery."

Since I had told Bok two things about Friedmann that I had not intended to tell, I bit my tongue and successfully held back the third: Friedmann's discovery. I had revealed to Bok that Friedmann was poor and physically disabled. Bok had not struck me as a man with a penchant for humor or aesthetics. So I did not tell him about the original music of the Hebrew alphabet. Bok might even suppose that in addition to being poor and sick—two strikes against a new-found relation—Friedmann was also mad. Who knows? Perhaps he already suspected something was wrong with a man who had waited more than twenty-eight years to seek out long-lost relatives. Perhaps for my idée fixe in bringing them together he even suspected me of the same thing. I knew that instead of increasing his faith in me, that foolish impersonation of a physician had diminished my credibility. But I had fulfilled my part of the bargain: I'd found Friedmann's relatives. I hadn't promised that his relatives would write to him, or like him, or send him money, or send for him. I'd promised to *find* them, and that promise I had kept. Now it was Friedmann's turn to keep his end of the bargain, and give me more information on the eighth wonder of the world.

I soon discovered that Friedmann had kept more of the bargain than I'd anticipated. To my surprise and joy, my travel grant to Budapest was approved, and my contract at the college was renewed for another year.

In June I was in Budapest again, wandering into that secluded *kehilla* courtyard, past the outdoor wrought iron marriage canopy, where I hoped to find Friedmann and the original music of the Hebrew alphabet.

IV

After lunch, I met Friedmann, hat tilted to the back of his head, waiting by the concrete pillar, scanning the occasional tourist who walked by. He greeted me as if he had expected me, and took my hand with obvious pleasure. "Ah, Doctor Gantz, I knew you'd be back. Come. I have much to tell you."

We walked slowly to his house without saying a word. I saw with what effort he limped and what will—yes, I repeat: iron will—it took to climb the four flights.

Friedmann hadn't changed; neither had his apartment. One table, one chair, and a cabinet on the wall. The cartons and packages—filled with coffee grounds, paper money, moonlight?—were still scattered on the floor.

"Please sit down. I am going to tell you a story."

"I will stand if you do."

"As you wish."

And before I had a chance of asking him how he was and what he'd done during the year, Friedmann began to speak.

"The story is like this. Some years ago, I do not remember how many, in peaceful days before the war, I was walking in the fields near Debrecen. It was a quiet, beautiful spring day. I think it was May or June. I felt as if I were in a nineteenth-century idyllic story. You know, something out of the early Hesse, or Grillparzer, or Robert Musil. Have you read Musil?"

"No. I never heard of him."

"Hesse?"

"Oh yes. Of course."

"He's probably fashionable in America. What about Adalbert Stifter?"

"Shtifter?"

"Yes, Stifter."

"No."

"No again? You should become acquainted with middle European literature. There is a certain atmosphere in these writers not reproduced elsewhere. Most people consider themselves cultured if they read"—here he pointed to the East—"Dostoevsky"—and, pointing to the West—"Maupassant and Dickens. But the vast span of Middle Europe they neglect."

"I hope to make good this remission as soon as I get back."

"It will certainly be to your profit . . . Well, to return. It was a perfect combination of personal mood, weather, and countryside. Two variables: mood and weather. One invariable: the tranquil scenery. I stopped to breathe. I heard a bird. Then I *thought* I heard a bird, singing a melody I have never heard before, for a bird does not have such melodic range. I cupped my hand to my ear. Did you ever have a feeling that you are experiencing something unique, something that will not happen again, and that at the moment you are experiencing it, shivers roll over you? Well, it was a man singing to himself. An old peasant. I stopped and listened until he finished. Then I approached and asked him

what he had been singing. He was apparently somewhat deaf and did not hear me. What sort of words
were these? thought I, as the melody went through my
mind. But when I extracted, pardon, *extricated* myself
long enough from the spell of the enchanting melody, I
realized he had not been singing words, but was reciting. Do you know what this old goy with the peasant
outfit I thought they stopped wearing sixty years ago
was reciting?"

"No," I said slowly. "I don't. Unless of course you
mean this as a rhetorical question."

Friedmann disregarded my interruption. "He had a
thick white mustache curled up at the ends like a hussar, and a sash about his waist, as though he had just
alighted from his horse. You know what this old hussar
was singing?"

This time I did not reply.

"The Hebrew alphabet."

And Friedmann began a dialogue, changing accent
as he mimicked the hussar:

"'Do you know Hebrew?' I asked him.

"He laughed. 'No. I do not know Hebrew.'

"'Do you know you are singing the Hebrew alphabet?'

"'That I do!'

"'Where did you learn it?'

"'Oh, a long time ago. Sixty years.'

"'I said where. Not when.'

"'Heard you. I am not deaf,' he said.

"'You probably grew up in a Jewish village, and used
to help light the stove in the schoolhouse and there you
learned the alphabet.'

"'No.'

"'Then please tell me.'

"'I got the melody in exchange.'

"'From whom?'

"'A holy man. Hasid rabbi. For a shepherd's song he heard me singing.'

"'Can you teach it to me? I too collect beautiful music.'

"'No. I forgot it. Like he said I would. He wanted it only for the holy prayers. Lost. Like the notes that dribble out of the fife.'

"'And he gave you the melody of the alphabet?' I asked.

"'Yes. That he did. He told me he would give me a secret. Something that had been passed from his grandfather's grandfather back to the angel Raziel. But to me he gave it.'

"'Why?'

"'Because he knew that I knew no Jews. He said he had no sons and there were too many quarrels in his circle of churchgoers.'

"'Do you know what you were singing?'

"'Yes. The Hebrew alphabet.'

"'For each letter another tune.'

"'You said it, not I. It is the lost music of the original alphabet. And I, a Christian,' he laughed, 'know the secret!'

"'Teach it to me.'

"'No. I will lose this melody too.'

"'You will not. I am from the family of the holy angel Raziel. My name too is Raziel. Lend me the melody.'

"'No. I will forget the melody.'

"'I promise you will not lose it. Look. You light a match and give of your fire to a friend who also smokes a pipe. Does your flame become smaller? No. Is it taken away? No. The melody you give is like fire. You will not forget your songs.'

"But the peasant shook his head.

"'Then I will sing you the melody I heard before to prove that I belong to the Raziel family, but you only tell me if I have sung it correctly.'

"The peasant agreed and I sang several letters of the melody for him.

"'Holy saints,' he said in excitement. 'A miracle!'

"'No miracle,' I said. 'I listen once and absorb melody. If you blow a note on your fife even without my looking I can tell you what note it is.'

"But instead of admiring this ability of mine, the old peasant muttered:

"'Witchcraft. Leave it to the Jews. First they make me forget my song and now they copy my alphabet music like a mirror. The village priest is right,' he said without anger, 'the devil is in the Jews.'

"And without another word, he walked away."

"And that, my dear friend Doctor Gantz, is the story of how I acquired the original music of the Hebrew alphabet."

The time had now come to make my request. By telling me the story, Friedmann had shown his trust in me. Now I knew he would be ready to show me the music.

"May I see it, Engineer Friedmann?" I asked with a tremor in my voice.

But Friedmann spread his crooked hands, tilted his head, and glowed his smile at me. "I cannot say that I am prepared now, that is, today. I must speak to my partner, Fürer."

"But I thought you promised . . ."

"I keep my promises, Doctor." Friedmann's bright penetrating eyes set into me. "That will be a mere formality, but though I am prepared to have you experience the music, I do not know if *you* are. I would like you to know more about the spirit of the letters."

His back turned to me, Friedmann opened up a bundle on the floor—one of perhaps a dozen different-sized cartons and soft, string-wrapped paper packages—took out a sheet of paper, straightened up, and began to read.

"There is a mysterious link between the aleph-beys and the universe we live in. The basic elements"—here Friedmann looked up—"I speak not of the periodic table of ninety-six or more elements of which I am well aware, but of universal basics, which primitive and modern man alike knew, and which the philosophers described for us . . . They are water, earth, fire. Each has its corresponding influence with a letter of the aleph-bet. Water is *mayim* in Hebrew; its link is the letter *mem,* which appears twice in the word *mayim;* the hissing *shin* is reminiscent of the hissing fire, *esh* in Hebrew; and the silent *aleph,* first born of the alphabet, first to be created, begins the word for *adamah,* earth, whence Adam was formed. Moreover, in the Hebrew aleph-bet there are seven doubled letters. These correspond to the seven planets . . ."

"But there are—"

"I anticipate your complaint. I know there are nine, but we must work from the knowledge of the ancients, when the philosophy of corresponding sciences was developed. So then, three elements, seven days of week, seven planets, and seven orifices of the body. Three plus seven is ten.

"Now there remain twelve plain letters with which

the twelve constellations were created. The letters, then, are not only symbols, but the elements and building materials of God's creative word—the basic forms of everything that exists. Pay heed: twelve letters, twelve notes, twelve tribes, twelve months. Tribes, space; months, time. The magic number is, will always be, twenty-two. Twelve notes out of which all music grows, and then ten numbers out of which all numbers grow. Remember too the ten moral numbers, the commandments, out of which all common law grows, for we can have no nature, no reality, no culture, without law. The ten and twelve yield twenty-two letters out of which all words, knowledge, destiny grow."

As Friedmann spoke of the alphabet he looked youthful, angelic, virginal—unsullied by this world. This virginality of his haunted me, even back in America. I had wanted to ask him a question, but was held back by tact. Now I decided to ask.

"Engineer Friedmann, I'd like to ask you a personal question."

He looked up at me and spread his crooked hands, waiting.

"Have you ever been kissed by a woman?"

Friedmann looked down at his hands and legs, as if to display himself as his answer. Then he gazed up at me, his face shining. Perhaps there was even a tear in the corner of one eye, I don't remember.

"Your question is more to confirm a formed supposition. Nevertheless, I shall answer you. Since it is something I have not experienced, I consider myself a master in imagination. A perfect critic. The answer is no. But there is a certain beauty in *not* experiencing something, not so Herr Doctor? Once someone, to poke fun at me for keeping kashrut, said: 'Why don't you try bacon, just once? You don't know how delicious it is.' My reply was: 'You do not know how delicious it is not.'

"But such subtlety is lost on people like that. But I can imagine how powerful, how intense can be the kiss of a woman, like the kiss of God. Unbearable. One might not survive it. But now I know why I can bear the beauty, the intensity of the melody of the Hebrew alphabet. *Because* I have never been kissed, there is enough reserve physical strength in me to absorb this severe metaphysical shock. If I would have been another—and had the kiss of a woman, God, goddess— the melody for me would have been like standing squarely in the path of a bolt of lightning."

"Are you suggesting that someone else, who has been kissed by women, might not be able to survive it? That I won't be able to withstand it?"

"I am not a physician. Only, in all modesty, a metaphysician. I shall ask Fürer what he thinks."

"When will you see him? I won't remain in Budapest too long you know."

"Perhaps tomorrow. Me you can always find at the *kehilla* kitchen . . . And now, I shall continue. Just as every Hebrew letter has a different shape, even a different feel, like raised or block letters, even different size— some are bigger, some weigh more—ask a typesetter— some are simple, like the letter *i,* some complex, like *q* or *g,* so each Hebrew letter has its own melody . . . Do you have a favorite letter?" Friedmann suddenly asked me.

"I haven't thought of it," I said.

"*Ayin,* for instance, is my favorite letter. Not in print. In script. The way it starts at one end—you are Jewish, aren't you?"

"Of course."

48

"It loops around itself and ends on the other side. Perfectly balanced. Standing on an egg, crossed arms up. There is a magnificent rhythm in the written letters, even a structural leitmotif, as if the aleph-beys were an artistically realized composition. The basic form of most letters is a semicircle. A circle divided by a NW to SE line at a 45° angle. Here"—Friedmann rushed to the cabinet, otherwise empty: I saw make-believe cups dangling on nonexistent hooks. He took out a pencil and paper—"I shall draw it for you. Like this, see? This top part, there you have it. This is the basic form of about half the aleph-beys, its continuing rhythm . . . The *ayin* does not have it. Maybe"—he put a finger to his cheek—"maybe *that* is why I like it. It is shaped differently. It has the courage to be different. Look again. Beautiful, not so, Herr Doctor? . . ."

I nodded.

"You really do not have a favorite letter?"

"No. I really don't think so. They all speak to me."

"Sing. *Sing.* You mean sing," he piped up at me, bobbing syncopatedly on his toes. "Now you wouldn't want to make me angry." And he flashed that cherubic smile. "The Hebrew letters *sing* . . . Don't forget that. Do you know why I like the letter *ayin?*"

"You told me. Because of its shape; its courage."

"I know I told you. But there is another reason. From another level of meaning. Because of its sound, its . . . how do you say in English, play on words?"

"Pun."

"Pun. Yes. Pun. Ah, that's it. Pun, fun. Grimm's law. Latin *pater,* German *fater*—you know. Not so?"

"I agree."

"You must be thirsty," Friedmann said.

"Not really."

"Good! I still do not have any supplies. I am sorry, my electric ring is as yet broken. Of late I dine out more frequently."

"That's perfectly all right."

"As I was saying," he continued, unflustered by his aborted tea break, "there is another reason why I like *ayin*. Because of its pun meaning. *Ayin* means eye. Notion of seeing, of encompassing everything. And yet, when the sound *ayin* is spelled with an *aleph, ayin* means nothingness. The word exists, yet it represents nothingness. But its melody is most fascinating." Friedmann raised a bent finger. "So much for the sound. Now for the shape. Don't you like the perfect, flawless shape of the letters? I'm neither a scribe, nor the son of a scribe. This I regret. I wish I could have devoted my life to creating the shape of the sacred letters which other people will sing. But when I write Hebrew, I do it with a conscious pleasure. It borders on mystical ecstasy. That is all for today, dear Doctor, I am fatigued."

V

The following day I made an appointment to meet Professor Laszlo Geller of the Jewish Historical Institute, the only active Jewish school of higher learning behind the Iron Curtain. I learned that Geller is something of a hero, for he single-handedly maintains research in Jewish culture and history in Hungary, and in effect is sole guardian of the famed Fensterwald Collection of 333 incunabula and rare manuscripts (through Geller's help I was later to discover a hitherto unknown Renaissance song by a Jewish composer, written in tiny script on the title page of an illuminated Hagada). We talked for a while about his institute and his relationship with free world scholars, and then, pacing in his office, he began to speak of Friedmann:

"What you said in your letter is very interesting. Amazing in its coincidence. But I still maintain that the two of them are not quite all there. Believe me. I know them for years. Fürer is sound of body, but mad; Friedmann, *nebekh,* is crippled *and* mad. Well, have you been in contact with Friedmann?"

"Yes. I saw him yesterday."

"I admire your pertinacity. Have you ever met Fürer?"

"No. I only heard of him from Friedmann."

"Come here." He beckoned me to the window. "Look down there. See that short man with the Van Dyke beard? Wearing a blue beret. That's him. He waits for me every morning. From seven-thirty. Four weeks already . . ." Geller nervously pressed his steel-rimmed glasses to his nose. "He is still there, waiting for me . . . Because of him I have to come and go via rear entrance, which fortunately he does not know exists . . . Tell me, do you really think the music of the aleph-beys is actual?"

"All this is new to me. It *sounds* impressive . . ."

"I just hope that you are not being naive."

"There is an interesting confluence of ideas in his remarks—a little too much divinity, of course, but—"

"Have you ever heard the music?" Geller looked as if he were teasing.

"No. Not yet."

"Neither has anyone else." Geller went to the telephone, lifted the receiver, then apparently changing his mind, replaced it.

"What do you think of it, Doctor Geller?"

"Well, it is Fürer's doings. His mind, his thought, his idée fixe—"

"I'm under the impression that Friedmann—"

Geller shook his head. "Friedmann, his best friend, helps him. They are in a league to perpetuate each other's"—Geller spread his hands—"fantasies. A society of the mad. My secretary told me that Fürer was constantly phoning me on an urgent matter. He had found the original music of the Hebrew alphabet. But I had had enough of madness. Budapest, you should know, is a convention of the mad: war survivors, survivors of attics, cellars, forests, sewers, survivors of death camps, labor camps, ghettos, survivors of torture." He lowered his voice. "Survivors of fascism, nazism, communism. Budapest is the basket that catches them all. They congregate here from all the villages, hoping that Budapest, like England for the melancholy Dane Hamlet, will cure them. That is why I told my secretary to tell Fürer I was not in. He stopped phoning. I thanked God. Too soon. Fürer started waiting at the entrance. He watches for me from seven-thirty in the morning, and waits patiently until ten. I had to begin using the rear entrance, going through a not-often-used courtyard. All right. Enough of this. Come, let me show you some of the Jewish sites of Budapest . . . This way to the rear stairs, please. Follow me."

We started the descent from the third floor. After one flight, Geller leaned over the railing and saw someone on the ground floor.

"Oh my God," he whispered. "Friedmann! Well, it's either him here, or Fürer there. Let's go. The poor man must have walked an hour to get here. I'm sure he cannot afford a taxi."

"Ah, Professor Geller," Friedmann said, and then spotting me, exclaimed: "And you too Doctor Gantz, what good fortune!"

"Good morning, Engineer Friedmann," Geller said, "To what do I owe this honor?"

"Please, Herr Professor. I have something to show you." Friedmann breathed heavily. His shirt, the hat band on his fedora, were wet with perspiration. But as usual he had on his broad, boyish smile. "Outside. I made great effort to come here." He lifted a finger that told us to wait. "It is outside."

Friedmann hobbled out. Geller shrugged. I sat down on the steps. Perhaps Friedmann had dragged one of his packages here to make his presentation. A minute later the door opened and Fürer ran in.

Fürer began in Hungarian, but seeing me—tipped off no doubt by Friedmann—he switched to English. Unlike Friedmann's clear baritone, Fürer had a tremulous, high-pitched voice.

"Aha! So there you are." He opened the door halfway and shouted, "Ferdinand! He's here!" Geller turned to the stairs as if to flee and then stopped, one foot resting on the first step.

Fürer, somewhat taller than Friedmann, took a deep breath and stood with his chest puffed out. He had a broad, high forehead and a little triangular chin-beard, which he combed and teased with his fingers. Lines etched deeply on either side of his thick lips gave his face a tragic cast. Fürer held the door open for Friedmann, who was beaming. Victory. A smile of pure bliss. He had engineered successfully the Fürer-Geller meeting.

"Doctor Gantz," Friedmann said. "I want to introduce you to my colleague, Ferenc Fürer."

We shook hands and I acknowledged the honor.

Fürer turned to Geller and began again in Hungarian, a rapid, high-pitched, whining speech.

"Ferenc, my dear," Friedmann held his friend's shoulder. "I must interrupt you. I beg you to speak the English language, so that my good friend and associate, Doctor Gantz, may understand."

Fürer cleared his throat, adjusted his beret, and began again.

"Herr Professor, I have been waiting so long to see you. Why did I call so many times and not find you in, not even once? You must be very busy, for you are never in your office. Why have I waited for you since early in the morning for four weeks now to great"—he leaned and whispered to Friedmann's ear, who in turn said something to Fürer—"inconvenience to myself, having to rise so early and wash and dress and eat before my usual hour of rising and washing and dressing and eating and you are never in your office because you are so busy elsewhere? Because I have something very important for you."

"The original music of the aleph-beys," Geller said.

"Your secretary told you. A reliable woman."

"But Mister Fürer, please—"

"*Doctor* Fürer."

"Doctor Fürer, excuse me. You have a doctorate?"

"Of course. The University of Vienna, Doctor of Jurisprudence. But owing to the turn of history, I neglected that field and devoted myself, *ourselves*"—he threw a smile at Friedmann—"to other affairs."

"Doctor Fürer, please understand that I will be very happy for you, for myself, for all of Israel, if you have indeed discovered what you say you have discovered. But music is not one of my specialties. So you are knocking, obstinately, stubbornly, if you will forgive my saying so, at the wrong door. I can hardly sing the Kiddush without drifting off key . . ."

Fürer put his hand into his jacket pocket and withdrew a bulging soiled white envelope. In it was a handwritten manuscript.

"I shall read you only a part of it. When it comes to the music, Friedmann will sing, for I no longer carry a melody well either. Have you ever heard Friedmann sing?"

"I confess I have not," Geller said.

"Neither have I had the pleasure," I added.

"Ferdinand has a voice like an angel."

"From the Raziel family," said Friedmann happily. "A matter of genes." Professor Geller glanced quickly at me as if to say: See what I mean? But I did not respond.

Geller looked at his watch. "A thousand pardons, but I am not the man for you. I must go now. I appreciate the honor—"

"But you are making a big mistake, Professor Geller. Wait! *I* waited so long. I displayed patience for four weeks. Please, you be patient for fourteen minutes. You cannot leave us now. In the history of culture there have always been astounding discoveries."

How remarkable, I thought. These were almost the very words I had written to Doctor Geller.

"They were never acknowledged immediately. The Rosetta Stone was held to be a forgery. Grimm's law was rejected. The Mayan inscriptions were considered the work of charlatans, fools. I could go on. Consider, consider . . ."

"I cannot abide it any longer," Geller burst out. "Coffee grounds. Energy from moonlight—"

"No. Moonlight is not our project," Fürer shouted.

"You are mixing up us with someone else," said Friedmann.

"—edible paper money," Geller continued. "Alphabet music. Please, please leave me alone. There are many people I have to take care of."

Fürer and Friedmann looked at me.

"I wrote to you, Professor Geller," I finally blurted out. "In America they discovered a new process for making paper from coffee grounds."

"Another one of our ideas stolen, Ferdinand," Fürer said.

"Wait," I said. "Edible paper has long been used in espionage. Because of the energy crisis the U.S. Space Agency is working on harnessing the energy of moonlight."

"I said moonlight is not our project," Fürer shouted again.

Friedmann shook his head. "We do not keep moonlight in water barrels like the fools of Chelm."

Then Fürer raised a warning finger to Geller. "We have something important here. Would you be happier if this would be acknowledged after my death?"

"No, no," said Geller quickly.

"I would be willing to die for this, so deeply do I believe in it." Fürer looked at Friedmann. "You too Ferdinand, not so?"

Friedmann hesitated. "I shall give my right hand in belief thereof," he said solemnly. "If I forget thee, O Jerusalem . . . But no death. No dying."

"Look, gentlemen," Geller said. "I have an idea. I shall send you to Professor Imre Kertesz. If he says it is worthwhile, I will gladly listen to your lecture."

"With Ferdinand singing?"

"Of course."

"Naturally," I added. "Wouldn't one expect Engineer Friedmann to sing it? After all, he heard it first during that famous walk in the fields near Debrecen."

"Oh no," Fürer said gently. "So you told him that, Ferdinand?" Then he turned to Doctor Geller. "It didn't happen to him. It happened to *me*."

"No, Ferenc, it happened to *me*."

"Friedmann thinks it happened to him because he has heard it so often he assumes it is *his* story."

"Then why is it that *I* know the melody?" Friedmann asked.

"Because I taught it to you, then forgot it. Or because since we all heard it at Sinai, when Moses sang his famous song, that is why you know it too."

"A very interesting argument, Ferenc, but for your information I *was* present. And it *is* my story. It was a day in May or June. I distinctly remember the weather in the outskirts of Debrecen."

"Ferdinand, my colleague and friend, I don't think we should argue. We agreed not to argue about this point."

"True, Ferenc, that is our agreement. And with the statement that in the first place it *is* my story and in the second place that you yourself, Fürer, told me that the story did not happen to you either but that you heard it from someone else, I consider out little dispute closed."

At which Friedmann clapped his hands and swiftly turned his face to me as though turning a page to a new chapter.

"Yes, indeed," Professor Geller said, with an ironic smile, "With Friedmann singing. And if it is authentic I shall have it taught to the synagogue choir. We shall give a public concert. I shall publish an article about you in the *kehilla* newspaper. We shall record it."

"No," Fürer said solemnly. "No recordings."

"I shall call Kertesz for an appointment. He'll write you. In two weeks, come back to me."

"Front entrance or back?" Fürer could not resist asking.

Geller disregarded the question. "And you shall tell me what Kertesz said."

Friedmann bowed; Fürer nodded. Arm in arm, they walked out the door.

"Who is Professor Kertesz?" I asked Geller.

"The greatest musicologist in Hungary."

"I've never heard of him—"

"Well, he hasn't published in fifteen or so years, but claims to be working on something important. He loves to drop broad hints about it, that sly old fox—he's eighty-three or -four now—but he will not answer a question, except with a finger-wagging, eyebrow-raising, 'Aha, uh-um.' He is usually a very gentle and courteous old man, but quite high strung when he is under pressure or when his tranquility is disturbed."

"Won't Friedmann and Fürer disturb his tranquility?"

"I do not think so. He may find some amusement in their *meshugass*. And if there is anything to their story he may even learn something. For he's a first-rate scholar and musician, but—"

"But what?"

Geller looked innocent.

"It's something juicy, right?" I said.

"Juicy? What is meaning of juicy?"

"Gossip. A scandal."

"Well, between you and me, early in Kertesz's career there was some talk of scandal. Blown out of proportion. Not even worth discussing."

"The wife of a musician?" I asked.

"No, not quite."

"The musician's daughter. He was after the daughter and seduced the wife."

"You have a very fecund, perhaps over-ripe imagination, Doctor Gantz. I can see what images the word 'skandal' conjures up among academicians in America. No, I am referring to something serious. Early in his career there was some foolish rumor that what had been considered a major article was actually written by a young associate."

"Plagiarism."

"Again, not quite. But arrogation of intellectual property. It had never been proven, for his loyal assistant—he died in the First World War—a brilliant composer and musicologist in his own right—never breathed a word. By the way, do you compose or play an instrument?"

"Neither." I tried not to answer stiffly. "I am solely devoted to musicology."

"Ah yes. Like Kertesz."

"Is he Jewish?"

"Of course. A perfect Galitzyaner. Born in a small town in Poland and brought here when he was six."

"Then wait a minute, Professor Geller," I said. "Then *he'll* take the idea."

"Don't be absurd. When there is zero there is nothing to take."

"But Friedmann promised me. . . . Excuse me . . ."

"Where are you going? What about our tour?"

"Pardon," I said over my shoulder. "Some other time. Excuse me, I must find Friedmann before it's too late."

I ran out, turned up the block, raced past dingy grey buildings. But I couldn't find them. They must have taken a taxi, I thought, as I myself entered one and directed the driver to Friedmann's apartment. Up, gasping, to the fourth floor. Locked. No answer. I ran to the communal kitchen, but Madame Dalno did not know where Friedmann was. She had not seen him at all.

A day later, I found Friedmann at his usual place.

"Engineer Friedmann," I said breathlessly. "Why did you go to Kertesz? You promised this information to me."

"I did it for you. To give it greater respectability."

"Did you see him?"

Friedmann seemed excited, but did not reply directly.

"It is only correct protocol to tell Professor Geller first, since he was instrumental in the arrangement. Come."

We walked to a store around the corner and phoned Doctor Geller, who told us to see him at ten the following morning.

"I cannot imagine they have seen him," Geller told me as we waited for Friedmann and his friend. "I did not even have a chance to call Kertesz."

"Friedmann was very excited. They probably saw him," I said.

The secretary buzzed. "The guests of honor have arrived," Geller said.

The door opened and the two came in. Fürer enthusiastically shook Geller's hand and mine.

"You saw Kertesz?" Geller asked, incredulous.

"Yes, yes," Fürer said. "Of course!"

"Thank you, Doctor Geller, for arranging it," Friedmann added.

"But I did not even have a chance to call!" Geller said. "How did—"

"*I* called," Fürer said, "and told him you sent us to him. We wanted to waste no time."

"And you told him all about your discovery?" Geller asked.

"I did," said Fürer. "Not only did I tell him. I showed him everything. I told him the whole story—"

"And he listened to you?"

"Yes, intently."

"Kertesz is a very polite man," Friedmann said.

"And you sang for him?" Geller asked.

"He invited Friedmann to sing."

"Yes," Friedmann nodded happily. "He invited me."

The virginality melted from his face. I felt betrayed.

"Without Friedmann," Fürer said, "without Friedmann's singing, the entire lecture is worth nil. Only Friedmann has the melody."

"And you gave him the melody?" I cried.

"And you?" Geller asked Fürer.

"Me? I know the theory."

"And the old man listened to all this patiently," Geller said.

"And how! He was fascinated."

Geller shook his head. "Old Kertesz has mellowed. Amazing!"

"And you gave him the melody?" I asked Friedmann again.

"He was quite . . . quite . . ." Fürer hesitated.

"Courteous," Friedmann concluded for him, adding, "You see, he believed in us. I sang for him. Twice. First time he did not hear me."

"Twice?" I shouted.

"Friedmann really did not want to sing it a second time."

"I have never sung it twice. It takes too much strength out of me. I am not a strong man. . . . But— since the professor musicologist requested it, I did him a favor."

"A favor!" Fürer exclaimed. "Friedmann, you are too—"

Here, once more, Fürer bent to Friedmann's ear, cupped it in his hand and whispered to him. Friedmann did the same to Fürer.

"—modest! An honor! Ferdinand, you did Kertesz an honor. You honored him by singing it a second time. Even for the first time."

Friedmann smiled modestly.

Professor Geller's lips moved, about to ask a question. He held back politely, however, as though someone had just begun to speak. But no one said a word. Finally, Geller asked:

"And . . . and what did Kertesz say in conclusion?"

"You mean when I finished my lecture?"

"When I finished singing?"

"Yes, gentlemen, what was the professor's opinion of your research, your discovery?"

"You don't know what he said?"

"You don't know what he thought of us?"

"How should I know, Friedmann? I have not spoken to Kertesz even to make the appointment for you. I have not spoken to him in months."

Here Fürer began quaking and smiling, beaming, bouncing on his toes; a tremor running through his hands made his fingers rattle as though loose. "Kertesz said, Kertesz said . . ." and here Fürer began laughing, looking at Friedmann.

"The professor of music . . ." Friedmann grinned. His large, liquid lips spread until his teeth—his radiant smile—covered most of his face. His eyes glittered with joy; tears filmed them. His face began quivering. The smile filled him. He moved up and down on his bandied legs until he looked like a grandfather clock tipping and turning, chiming with laughter. I expected a cuckoo to caw. Friedmann's hands, the hands of that imaginary clock, began to tremble. "The professor said . . ." Friedmann chanted, his hands shaking, eyes blinking, tears streaming. Friedmann now went into the full paroxysm of machine-like movement, face, hands, body, feet bobbing crookedly up and down—voice all aquiver, aflame, infused with laughter, sobs, and giggles, and a high-pitched utterance: "He said, I am —"

"*We* are" — Fürer now joined in.

My head spun. Nothing was still. I was thrust into a blow-up of Matisse's *The Red Room*. Everything in mind-reeling amber vibration.

"*Meshugge!*" they both chanted.

"*Totally meshugge,*" Fürer sang triumphantly.

"Mazel tov," Geller said dryly. With a formal bow, he shook Fürer's hand, then Friedmann's. I placed my hands behind my back. "I am delighted that Professor Kertesz and I are in perfect agreement."

Silence. Dead stock still. No clock ticked. A crack in the wall moving softly along the plaster was the only sound I heard. A voice urged me to tell Friedmann: "It isn't so." But I only whispered, barely audibly: "I don't believe it."

For I was in a quandary, a perfect paradox. If they were mad, then the original music of the Hebrew alphabet did not exist; and if they were not, then the music was no longer mine.

VI

"Engineer Friedmann?" I asked, knocking on the open door.

Again the kitchen was empty.

"Friedmann?" I called. "Engineer Friedmann, are you home? It's me."

"Yes," I heard from behind a door, "and no."

And he emerged, not formally clothed in his Sabbath outfit, but almost naked, except for the fedora on his head and a long-sleeved white nightshirt that hung just over his hipbones.

I was so surprised at his attire, I did not know what to say.

I had thought of talking to him about the implications of his visit to Kertesz; yet I was afraid it might spoil my chances for hearing the music of the alphabet.

"Look," Friedmann began without any small talk, as if by common consent this was the sole purpose of my visit. "See this note?"

He showed me a C on a sheet of music that he had drawn.

"Of course."

"Sing it."

I did.

"Good. And this one?"

I sang an A.

"And this?"

"That's a B." I sang that, too, trying not to laugh. Friedmann stood there, this raggedy philosopher, in his short nightshirt—one wrong move and his testicles would show—giving me my first music lesson.

"All right. You have just sung A, B, C. Do you know what you have done? You have begun the alphabet. You have described musically three letters. But since Hebrew is an older language, the melody is more complex. We all recognize letters. They are symbols. Show an *A* almost all over the world and people will sing the same note—violins, oboes, all over the world, vibrate to the same frequency. If an A can have a certain tone, surely it can apply to the Hebrew alphabet, the world's first alphabet, where letters are so closely bound to poetry and poetry to *trop* and music. You see, for instance, a name has music, a characteristic all its own. When you mention someone's name, a certain image, a musical sensation comes to mind. This is not only because of the personality but also because of the letters and the combination of sounds."

Friedmann pulled the chair out for me. Usually both of us stood, with Friedmann leaning against the unused chair. Now he insisted that I sit.

"The sun is the source of light. One can appreciate it indirectly. If we stay out too long in the sun, its rays will harm us. In like fashion, we cannot bear the original melody of the Hebrew alphabet. It is too powerful, too unbearable, like gazing directly at sunlight."

Friedmann's words disturbed me. I thought he might be wanting to squirm out of his promise.

"You hinted once before, Engineer Friedmann, that because I've been kissed by a woman I won't be able to

66

withstand the melody. But I *shall.* What the old peasant could stand, I can stand. If old Kertesz could, I certainly can."

"I do not wish to go into that now."

"So if you wish to sing for me, please do."

"If so, I shall now sing for you the music, the original melody for each letter of the Hebrew aleph-bet."

A rill of shivers waved over me. I felt a burst of bright sunlight I could not see.

Friedmann began—I did not believe it was happening. I didn't believe he would begin so suddenly—then stopped. What further teasing, torture, endless waiting, crossing of Rubicons, would he impose on me? Would the wizard in my envisioned fantasy, my fairy tale, snatch away my princess once more?

"You are uncomfortable, Doctor. You are perspiring. Your fingers are nervously doing a quadrille in your jacket. It is too hot here for a jacket, Doctor Gantz. Why do you wear it?"

"I'm chilly, Engineer Friedmann."

"Nonsense. You are perspiring."

"No. It's quite all right."

"I cannot sing if I believe you to be uncomfortable. Here, let me have your jacket."

He tugged at my lapel with one hand, and at the sleeve with his other hand. I complied.

"Put the jacket on the chair, please, Engineer Friedmann."

"No. It may get soiled here. I shall place it in my other room."

"Fine, then I'll just remove this packet of cigarettes."

"But I cannot abide smoke. If you wish me to undergo strain of singing the alphabet I must be at ease. Smoke makes me cough."

"But I won't smoke."

"No matter. Even the appearance of a packet of cigarettes makes me ill. I am being polite. I do not wish to focus on that little packet you have there and are gingering so fingerly . . . See! In my excitement you are making me metathesize! That is why I shall not sing if that little packet of cigarettes is there. I shall place your jacket in the other room."

I sighed.

Eyes closed, Friedmann began to sing. He had a ringingly clear beautiful baritone. I had not realized that from a body like his such sounds could come. His face shone; he looked angelic. He sang the first five letters. Each letter had its own tune, yet the melody was related to the letter than followed. The melody was haunting—it reverberates in my ears still, though re-creating it eludes me—but not without some anguish and intense pain, like a plethora of pleasure that one's sensibilities are not prepared for. I felt I had landed in an area of the unconscious—was I drugged?—where I listened with some inner ear that had links to the past. Not only was the melody lovely, modally pre-medieval, attesting to its ancientness; but in its formation, and in Friedmann's impeccable delivery, meticulous phrasing and modulation, it seemed to sculpt the form of the letter in the air. The sound of the *aleph,* for instance, *looked* like an *aleph,* starting at one high point and then descending in decrescendo—and then began, as it were, high on the opposite side again and continued with another downward glissando. The melody of the *bet* appeared lateral, then vertical, then lateral (the notes in reverse) once more, a miniature rondo. In general, the characteristics of the melody were a psalmodical recitative of a few tones (scarcely surpassing the trichord or tetrachord) with frequent symmetrical cadences and with a pure declamatoric rhythm, without any traces of that chromatic style which European consciousness knows nowadays as "Jewish" or "Eastern."

Suddenly Friedmann stopped. He opened his eyes, seemed to come down to earth. He wiped some drops of perspiration from his forehead.

"Nu?" he said. "It gives you the creeps?"

"I can't explain it."

"It reminds you of horses of fire, horses of darkness, galloping horses of iron?"

"Horses of fire, horses of light," I said.

"But something is bothering you."

"No. Please continue. I'm entranced. I've never heard melody like this. Ever."

Friedmann smiled thinly. "But your thoughts betray you. There is a certain lack of confidence in you. It radiates out and disturbs my intense concentration on the difficult melody. I sense it like a conductor with perfect pitch who hears false note in a hundred-voice chorus."

I admitted something was indeed troubling me.

"What is it?"

"Please don't be offended, Engineer Friedmann. I deeply appreciate what you are doing for me."

"And I have not forgotten that you found my relatives."

"But since you asked me, I want to know—what proof do you have that this is indeed the authentic, pristine, original music of the Hebrew alphabet? Don't even consider it *my* question. Consider it a question I shall undoubtedly be asked."

"Proof!" Friedmann moved excitedly on his toes.

"Rpoof!" he sputtered. "What rpoof do *you* have that *you* exist? Come, Herr Professor! Come, Herr Doktor!" This time he pronounced them in German. "Give me a footnote!"

"Even two. My passport and my birth certificate."

"Naive American!" Friedmann limped to a package on the floor, untied a string, brushed away my offer of help.

"Nonsense! Nonsense! Here! Look!" He waved an identity card with his picture. "Look. Aryan name. Ludwig Ignatz von Löckholz. Does this mean Löckholz exists? He was created to save me during the war. And for a while the card helped. So don't tell me about documents, documentation, footnotes, proof. The existence of the song is the existence of the song. Thank God, or whatever you believe in, that it does exist. It exists because the melody lives. It has been passed on from father to son."

"Who will you pass it on to? Do you have any children?"

He tilted the hat back on his head as though to reveal more of his forehead. "I have never married . . . Even though I am old enough to be your father."

"You . . . my father!"

"Correct . . . How old do you think I am?"

"At first I thought you were a youth, but now I realize you must be forty or forty-three, even though you don't look that old."

"More. Much more."

"Fifty?"

"More!" He laughed, pleased.

"I cannot guess. Tell me."

"I am on government pension."

"You're sixty-five?"

"I have been on pension for two years." Here he smiled and that boyish radiance once again suffused his face. "It is the melody that keeps me young. It is like the elixir of life."

"Do you intend to pass the music on to anyone?" I felt my heart pounding.

"It depends. We shall see. I have a partner to consult, you understand."

"Please continue," I asked.

"No. I think that will be all. You want too much documentation, Doctor Gantz. You have theory, interest, curiosity, but no fire. A handshake but no faith. No sefirot, no letters, no melody. You claim to be scientific, but yet you told my dear cousin Bok you consider finding him miraculous. So you do have some small faith after all."

"I don't deny I said that," I remarked, wondering why Bok was so keen on quoting me.

"Yet you still demand scholarly proof. Is not intuition enough?"

"Please. I shall give you money, Engineer Friedmann. All the money I have."

"But I don't need money. I have too many possessions as is."

"And I'll send you more if you give me, only me, the complete melody. This is what I've come for. This is what an important foundation has given me travel money to study, thus acknowledging the authenticity of your possession. Engineer Friedmann, my livelihood, my career, is at stake. Please! My very future. I don't want to drive a taxi. I don't want to work for the post office. Sell me the complete melody."

"No. I will not sell it. Nor will I give it, because you wanted to take it. Don't look so surprised. You think I am naive? You think that because I close my eyes and transport myself to realms far removed, that because I eat the stale fish that Madame Dalno occasionally serves that the cotton can be pulled over my eyes? That I do not know that all of a sudden you come in with packet cigarettes when I have never seen you smoking before? I may be mad, my dear Doctor Gantz, but I am not stupid. You wanted to record the melody secretly, without permission, on that little tape recorder which gives impression it is a packet of cigarettes."

"Only so I won't forget it. I apologize. I'm sorry I tried to fool you. You don't deserve it. You're a genius, Engineer Friedmann. I didn't want to flatter you. But Kertesz is dead wrong. I only wanted to record it for my own memory. Not to deny you. By no means. I swear it. You should see what I wrote about you, the noted Professor Doctor Ferdinand Friedmann, in my application for stipendium."

"The melody must be remembered. It is unforgettable."

"I'll bring you to the United States."

Here Friedmann gave a little involuntary twist to his body.

"I'll prepare an affidavit for you. I'll be your guarantor."

Friedmann leaned forward and clenched his twisted arm into a fist. "The human brain is not a saleable commodity. There are so many voracious fanciers of the human brain, who love to devour that food whether it be served pickled, or in a stew, or fricassee, that I should state here and now that the human brain cannot be bought and sold like so many pounds of coffee or a round of cheese."

"Did you make that up or are you quoting?"

"You are the musicologist, dear Doctor Gantz."

"It sounds familiar."

"It is from Beethoven's draft of a plan for a complete edition of his works. And I agree with my namesake Ludwig completely. Not for sale."

At a glance I took in the scene before me, viewing myself as though I were in the next room. I saw Friedmann, who stood almost naked except for a nightshirt, and young Doctor Gantz. What a hopeless, ridiculous morass I'd gotten myself into, had risked job and future and reputation for. *I* was mad. It was I who was the madman! Why shouldn't I tell him what I'd suspected long ago and had muttered to myself in bed at night: He'd taken me on the longest ride I'd ever been taken on.

"How do I know you're *not* Löckholz? Suppose you took over some Ferdinand Friedmann's identity, and thus acquired all his relatives? Suppose you're *not* Friedmann?"

"Does that disqualify, or make less potent, the original music of the Hebrew alphabet?"

"How do I know you're Jewish, in fact?"

Friedmann grew pale. The angelic smile soured as he looked at me—he rolled up one sleeve—but it still edged his wide lips, curving up like a rind of watermelon from eye to eye. "See the tattooed numbers. Auschwitz. Look carefully. And now this." And again he burrowed into a package, and emerged with another identity card issued by the Germans. "Check the numbers. Arms and card. Now do you believe? As for Jewish—"

He lifted up his white nightshirt.

My head reeled. I felt I was living in some avant garde audience participation play that violated my sense of privacy, my propriety, my dignity.

"During the war"—by now he had dropped his nightshirt, unruffled—"one was constantly afraid of being exposed—figuratively and literally. The goyim here are of course not circumcised. Catholics, one and all, and the bris was the covenant of death for many Jewish men. In the United States, I understand, almost all men are circumcised, gentile and Jew. That is good. A good sign, for it shows democracy at work; one's enemies cannot be singled out. But now, after war, what fear have I of exposing myself? I am conscious of the pun. I am proud I am a Jew . . . But you, Professor Gantz, still have no faith. You have clever insight, which I admire, but little faith."

"Forgive me. It has been a long journey. An incredible one. Friends back home won't believe half of what I'll tell them."

"Your friends lack faith too. Birds who have similar plumage congregate together."

"Your translation, Engineer Friedmann, is somewhat remiss. Birds of a feather flock together."

"Engineer Friedmann?" He turned around. "Who is that?"

"I am talking to you."

"But I am not Engineer Friedmann."

"What?"

"Very possibly I may even be you. Each man, present at Sinai, may have shifted person, persona, personality. All of us at one time or another are other people. Conscious imitation is the first step in this procedure. Unconscious imitation is the second. Just as we are other people in addition to ourselves, so are we the sum total of our past and future experiences. Like the letter *bet,* first letter of the Torah, lateral and vertical. To express it another way, there is no man who is not at each moment what he has been and what he will be."

"Then my hunch was right, Engineer Friedmann. I *thought* you might not be Friedmann but someone else."

"You are right. I am not the Friedmann, for I cannot imagine that God would punish a poor man like me with being crippled and having to eat at others' tables and having a mind and education that cannot be put to practical purposes. He did not do it to me. He would not. He did it to Friedmann, poor Friedmann who is already dead, so he certainly would not mind being crippled. For after all, is not crippled preferable to dead? Would not one want to come back crippled, like Friedmann, come back from the dead, for life is always preferable to death, not so, Herr Doctor?"

"I agree. I love life too . . . Forgive me for talking to you like this. I'm sorry. Thanks for everything." I shook his hand quickly and backed toward the door.

"Wait! Where are you going? I want to present you with a copy of the manuscript. To look through me and see I am not really Friedmann, only a man with an imagination could accomplish. It is too bad you are not a composer. You might have done well. I shall notate for you the music of the alphabet and send it to you."

"What about Kertesz?"

"I shall write you about him when I mail you the notations."

VII

All this took place in June; I spent July and August doing research in European libraries. On the plane back to New York, like the girl in the fable, I was counting my chicks. I had, or would have, everything I wanted. Manuscript, music, the works. With such a find, I could keep my job, make a stir in musical circles, and win a promotion too. Perhaps offers from other institutions. Fellowships for further study would now be quickly granted. Interviews with the media. Page one of the *New York Times*. And who knows what other literary spin-offs would accrue from this?

When I got home I went through the accumulated mail. There was a special delivery letter from Friedmann, and the latest issue of *The Musical Quarterly*, which I opened first, anxious to see if my review of the new edition of Adalbert Ignatius's *Early Renaissance Music in the Court of Spain* had appeared. There it was, with my name at the bottom of the cover. I imagined that perhaps in the Winter or Spring issue, my lead article would appear, titled, "The Original Music of the Hebrew Alphabet." I imagined it so powerfully, I created the letters, letters which as Friedmann said, have their own melody, their own form, their own weight and size, into the title swimming on the cover of

The Musical Quarterly. My eyes unfocused; the letters blurred. I tried to recreate the melody of the *aleph*— first letter of creation—my eyes cleared; the letters too. I rubbed my eyes, the title did not go. A pit opened beneath me, into which my heart, my soul, my entire being that could be loosened from the corporeal, fell. I saw: "The Original Music of the Hebrew Alphabet" by Professor Imre Kertesz.

In gloom, I opened up Friedmann's letter:

Dear Dr. Isaac Gantz:

You have probably found out by now the sad news that Kertesz deceived us. We were fooled. He called us *meshugge,* and Dr. Geller agreed, but in the meantime he took our work seriously. Kertesz tricked us, that nasty old Galitzyaner. Go have business with a man from Ayshishok.

But if it will make you happy—no, I *know* it will make you happy—I have better news for you. You will remember that Kertesz heard me sing the alphabet, and then, stating that he did not hear me well, asked me to sing again, which is very difficult for me to do, for I have to bring up and expend all physical and spiritual energy I posses in order to do this. But I did it for him. Not without suspicion, my dear Doctor, I hasten to assure you. In fact, when I sang for him the second time, I did *not* sing correct melody, for I suspected he asked me to repeat the strenuous and complicated set of melodies for the purposement of recording. And because of this experience I was especially wary, with eyes very wide open, and hence I was able to discern that you too had recording equipment. So instead of singing the correct melody, I sang some variations on Polish folksongs that my grandmother of blessed memory taught to me when I have been a child. So, if you wish, you may write to the magazine and thereby fulfill your publish or perish assignment and tell them the real melody which is on the manuscript that under separate cover will is on its way. Without doubt a clever musicologist-folklorist will identify the Polish tunes.

And remember, dear Doctor Gantz, may I call you Isaac? and from now on you call me Ferdinand or Avraham, remember that it is not I who sing the letters. I am just an instrument, the letters sing themselves through me. Do you know that marvelous metaphor that appears in the *Musaf* service of Rosh Hashana and Yom Kippur, where it states that God records the deeds of men and these deeds are recorded in a book "that reads itself"? It is one of the most memorable and fantastic images in all of literature. An image worthy of Borges or Absurdist Theater, which is what all of Budapest, nay, the entire twentieth century, is. Imagine! A book that reads itself. But that is not so surprising if one realizes that the Hebrew letters sing themselves. So now you know the mystical potency of the Hebrew letters, letters that have eyes with which they read themselves, letters that can sing of their own accord.

Your friend and colleague,
Ferdinand Friedmann, B.Sc.Eng.

Friedmann's odd combination of present and future, will is, in the next-to-last paragraph puzzled me. But I felt better. I began reading Kertesz's article which,

happily, was full of misinterpretations and misunder-
stood points. Reading it, I formulated my own article
in rebuttal, while hearing Friedmann's voice and the
ambiance of sanctity he created as he sang for me the
first five letters of the Hebrew alphabet. For hundreds
of generations the melody had not been publicly
known, but passed down from father to son, from family to family. I had heard the melody that Abraham had
sung, that King David chanted. Perhaps, then, I
thought, this song should *not* be known, but maintain
its silence, its anonymity, as it had during the past five
thousand years of the alphabet's existence. It had been
in my power to make it known to the public, but I had
a greater power in my possession: *not* to make it
known. The romantic in me urged silence. Something
indeed would be broken if the secret music of the Hebrew alphabet would be revealed, and hence, against
my professional judgment, I wished that I had not
learned it. Nevertheless, isn't there an element of destiny here? For we are what we are and what we will be,
like the sides of the letter *bet,* lateral and vertical,
present and future, will and is, will is. But then I
thought about transmission. Should it stop with Friedmann? Or me? Friedmann's Hebrew name is Abraham.
Mine, Isaac. On the other hand, perhaps just as Friedmann was not Friedmann, perhaps I—all of us actors
in a Theater of the Absurd—perhaps I was not Isaac
but Ishmael, caught stealing the original music of the
Hebrew alphabet, for which I'd be banished and have
the music taken away. If, as Friedmann said, everyone
at the same time may be both himself and someone
else, perhaps he was Friedmann, Löckholz, and the
nameless Jew he really was, and I was Isaac and Ishmael, both blessed by and punished for the original

music of the Hebrew alphabet, and perhaps I was Friedmann too. And even if the cycle would begin again, and I *were* the Isaac to his Abraham, how could I pass on a melody I had not heard completely and knew imperfectly? And which fairy tale prince would *I* tease and play the wizard to before I'd consent to give him the original music of the Hebrew alphabet, which I'd heard one lovely day while walking the fields near Debrecen? But if Friedmann was not Friedmann, then perhaps the melody was not real either, and just as Friedmann had sung Polish folktunes to Kertesz, perhaps he had sung other false songs to me too. But even though my intuition, my soul—the soul I do not deny, even though I am a doctor, a Ph.D.—tells me that I had had the privilege of listening to an ancient, unheard set of melodies—melodies the like of which are not to be found today—still there surfaces in me that nasty rpoof-seeking demon, insinuating his way through me, nibbling at my memory, enveloping like a merciless amoeba the few notes I still possess and cling to, and mice-sharp teeth gnawing at the letters of the aleph-beys until all the varying tunes of the original music sound like one, and all the letters look alike, a perfect circle divided by a NW to SE line at a 45° angle, o in Latin, *samekh* in the Hebrew alphabet, said *samekh* also standing for Satan, the perfect circle severed, much like the perfect, partial melodies of the Hebrew alphabet that David sang for Saul were severed by the spear the king cast in frustration at the fairy-tale king-to-be.

Weekend in Mustara

I

The Synagogue

Mustara lies high in the mountains, halfway between the snowcaps and the sea. The air is thin and clear—at sunset I often saw the water—and cool in summer, especially at night. I found the craggy zigzag peaks, visible everywhere in the city, both awesome and disconcerting, a kind of pressure on the soul.

Mustara has a surprising climate; all the travel books marvel at its fickleness and delights. Although the authorities have only recently opened their land to tourism, this fish-shaped island floating in an azure sea had long been noted by ancient and medieval travelers. Talmudic sages Rav Ulla and Mar Isak stopped here on their way to see the Emperor of Rome, and compared the merits of the local mountain air to that of Jerusalem. Centuries later, Marco Polo and Benjamin of Tudela noted the bazaar in their travelogues. Benjamin also noted Europe's oldest working pharmacy, and the world's foremost Jewish treasure: the fabled Hebrew Codex of the Bible, written in 891.

But although I did not close my eyes to the lovely landscapes—so reminiscent of Switzerland—I had not come to Mustara as a tourist. I did not come to scale the legendary peaks—mentioned in Near Eastern literatures, from Ugaritic to Minoan, from Coptic to

Sumerian—peaks that have eluded climbers for centuries, nor to photograph the Codex, which the authorities have strictly forbidden. I had not even come to set foot in the old pharmacy whose "centuries-old aromatic fragrances are steeped into its walls" (I quote the rapturous travel brochures). I *had* come in search of eleventh- and twelfth-century Hebrew manuscripts that no one had ever seen before.

My first Friday night here I left my little room in the neutrally named Pension Royale—its name had none of the exotic flavor of other places in Mustara, but it was located on a hillside and had a view of the sea — and walked along the main street. From there I turned into a side street, home of the outdoor pushcart market, and then, following a sign, to Synagogue Lane. I walked up the steep cobblestoned lane to the unmarked synagogue. I knew the address well, for I had written to the rabbi three times before my coming here.

In the large entrance hall I saw a remarkable mosaic floor. I traced its design with my eyes—men holding willows and palms, an angel holding a large scale of justice—and then descended seven wooden steps to the synagogue. I opened the heavy oaken door and walked in.

I had not seen a synagogue like this before. The Holy Ark—at the far end of the room—was made of marble but recessed into the Eastern wall. In the Italian fashion, sets of pews—men's section on one side, women's on the other—faced each other around an open central space on which lay a magnificent green oriental carpet. Most odd, however, was the position of the prayer leader. He did not stand in front of the Ark. There was no lectern before the Ark, and no bimah either;

instead, at the rear of the synagogue was an elaborately hand-carved wooden canopy, under which the rabbi stood, like a bridegroom waiting for his bride.

The rabbi swayed gently before a large oaken lectern that blended into the decor of the canopy. For a moment he turned away from the Siddur to look at me. The shamash, a swarthy, neatly dressed man, came up to me. As he handed me a Siddur, I noticed his tie was wrinkled and the top button of his white shirt was open. A faint smell of beer clung to him. He pointed to the seats on the right side, indicating that I should join the three men there.

I looked around. One of the men was standing, attending the rabbi's words. Opposite me, in the women's section, sat four thin, sad-faced old women. They looked like scions of old Jewish aristocracy. Were they four sisters or was one the mother? At the end of the row, two other ladies in American dress, smiling automatically at everyone, sat opposite their restless husbands whose pink skullcaps perched incongruously, like little pyramids, on their heads. The shamash himself did not pray, but stood respectfully at the side of the canopy, a few feet away from the rabbi.

The rabbi chanted a beautiful melody. The door opened. Another man with a two-day growth of beard came in. He had baggy blue trousers, his blue jacket was three shades darker, and he wore no tie; but one could see there was no breach of decorum intended. He stood with eyes closed for a moment, but when the shamash approached with a Siddur, the newcomer gently put his hand on the shamash's arm and declined. The four women, I noticed, averted their eyes from him as though his presence broke the air of piety and dignity. He scanned their faces, then those of the others. At me he looked once, then at the rabbi who nodded to him. I thought that surely he would wait to recite the Kaddish, but he left just as the rabbi was about to begin the hymn, "Come my beloved to greet the bride."

I watched the rabbi. Elated at being in Mustara, intrigued by this synagogue, I saw things through a cloud, as though I'd taken a heavy dose of cough medicine. My sensations of the rabbi shifted. First I saw only his face, his lips moving, but heard no sound. Then I heard only his clear baritone voice, singing the classical Hebrew prayers in the cantillic rhythms of the Italian rite. And then I neither saw nor heard him, but was just aware of his presence—colors and form, the idea of Jewish community in a land so long isolated—the rabbi of an ancient Jewish community mentioned in the Talmud and perhaps even hinted at in the biblical phrase "the island beyond." All I knew of the rabbi, who had not answered my three letters, was that he stemmed from a noted family of Italian rabbis and scholars, the Gagliatacozzos.

Was the rabbi as bad as he was made out to be by the American tourist I'd met the other day? The American was on his way down from Mustara, I on my way up. We met at the bus rest-stop midway between the port city, Kal'ir, and Mustara, where the drivers exchanged buses. The tourist talked about the Codex.

"They don't show it to nobody. You got to be Chief Rabbi or something to see it. You know what that shmuck in the State Museum offered me? Slides! Big deal! Slides I don't need to travel eight thousand miles for. And all those come-on brochures they put out in New York. Mustara—The Codex! As if it belonged to them."

"It does," I reminded him.

"It belongs to us," he said angrily, "the goyim are just holding it for us."

"Did you meet the rabbi?" I asked him.

"There's another lulu," the tourist snapped. "You got to hear about this Rabbi Gagliatoacozzi, or however you pronounce his name. I only spent eight or nine minutes with him, and if he didn't look at his watch six times, he didn't look once. What's your hurry, Rabbi, I told him? Got to catch the 5:21 to New York? But this he didn't get. No sense of humor. My Lord, my rabbi back home at Southport, who isn't the funniest chap in the world, got more humor in his *linke peye* than this rabbi with the Mafia name got in his whole body. Listen! I spend most of my free twelve hours of port call coming up to find out something about my people in far-off Mustara and this guy has no time to answer all my questions. You don't ask, you don't learn is my motto, right? I had a big donation in my pocket, but I didn't leave them a penny. No money for a rabbi who punches a time clock."

"Can you get antiques there?" I asked to change the subject.

"You interested in antiques?"

"Sort of," I replied.

"You play your cards pretty close to the vest, don't you?"

"What do you mean by that?"

"You're a pretty tight-lipped young feller, aren't you? You ask a million questions but don't even want to answer one for me."

"Come my beloved to greet the bride," chanted the rabbi. *"L'cha dodi li'krat kalla."*

The rabbi's voice lured me back to the prayers. Perhaps he chanted too rapidly, but the devotion was there. Sometimes his eyes were closed; when they were open, he gazed above the heads of the worshipers, at a point this side of infinity.

I shivered. Although it was June and pleasant outside, the synagogue was cold. We were below ground level. The walls were made of stone; heavy iron menorahs were suspended from the walls; and wrought-iron lamps provided chill illumination. There were no windows in the synagogue, even though the Talmud prescribed windows for a place of prayer. I had a bizarre thought. What if a bolt would slide and we were trapped eternally in this dungeon, our prayers congealed on our lips? If the Inquisition came and brought us all before the stake, burning our bodies while purifying our souls? I looked for the Eternal Light. Or if I could only have seen the sun; the sun too could have served as an Eternal Light.

The rabbi's melody echoed, bounced from stone to stone. I looked at the American tourists and felt reassured. What would the Inquisition want with them? Then, to my relief, I saw a tiny red light peeping out of a tightly woven iron lamp above the Holy Ark. The bolt unslid in my mind.

At the end of the service the congregants wished one another "Shabbat shalom." The rabbi bowed to each of the congregants. The two tourist ladies, all smiles, lingered for a moment, but had no common language with the rabbi who only knew a few words of English, or perhaps pretended ignorance. Their husbands raced out, stuffing their pink skullcaps into their trouser pockets like kids running out of Hebrew school. The rabbi reserved the greatest respect for the four old women. He shook hands with each of them, and exchanged greetings. When everyone was gone, he clasped my hand and said in Hebrew, "Shabbat shalom. You must be the young man who wrote two times to me."

"Three," I said.

"No matter. Two is just as bad. Please forgive me for not answering you but, as you know, a rabbi, especially here, is not master of his fate." He stopped, looked into my eyes, as if waiting for me to speak.

I had so many questions to ask. I did not know where to begin.

"It is especially difficult now," the rabbi said, "that the gates have been opened to tourists. They flood us. 'And the waters have encompassed my soul,'" he quoted the classical phrase from the Book of Psalms.

"Do they become a burden?"

"God forbid! *Kol Yisrael haverim.* All Israel are brethren. But now that ships dock in Kal'ir, the tourists take the bus up here for a quick tour of Jewish sites and ask questions to which they don't even have the patience to hear the answers. Still, they want to know everything about us. Do we keep kosher? Do we observe the Sabbath? Do we have evening courses? Am I circumcised? How many intermarriages were there last year? What is the anti-Semitism here like? Can they see the oldest member of the community?"

"You know, Rabbi, I understand their interest. It is only natural. I also wanted to ask you a few questions."

"Of course I don't mean you. You are not like that. You are not a two-hour tourist. I even had an interesting man here rushing in the other day who asked me to teach him the local dialect. How long do you have? He looked at his watch and said, 'My boat leaves in three hours, but I just want to learn some words and phrases so I can understand the jokes.' Now isn't that strange?"

I thought it was funny, but since the rabbi didn't even smile, I nodded sympathetically.

"Well, you have some interesting people here in your synagogue too."

"Ah, yes," the rabbi hesitated. "A history can be written around each of them."

I thought he would continue, but again he stopped. Down the hall, in rooms I could not see, I heard lights being flicked on, loud clicks resounding between the stone walls.

"Would you like to tell me about them?" I said.

Rabbi Gagliatacozzo shrugged. "For instance?"

"The man who hands out the Siddurim. I noticed he was not praying. Shamash, right?"

"But he is not a Jew. Dom Domingo is a Christian. He has taught himself to follow the prayers."

"Then there was a man who stood but did not pray."

"He is the president of our congregation. He does not know how to read."

"And the man who left soon after he came in?"

"Ah, yes! Menahem Piadadé. He comes for Shabbat services sometimes. Stems from an old family. Actually he is a cousin of the women you saw here, the Harreras, but between them relations are not good. Something to do with a quarrel fifty years ago—inheritance. Let us not recall it on the Sabbath, the day of shalom. Unfortunately, he is not well off."

"What sort of relationship do the women now have with their cousin?"

I saw that the rabbi was getting impatient. His wrist flicked, as though he were about to glance at his watch.

I knew I should not be asking him so many questions all at once, but I could not help myself: I wanted to know everything.

"Peace among families is a noble thing. Our sages teach us to be like the disciples of Aaron, loving peace and pursuing peace."

"Do they help him at all, do they support the synagogue?"

"Maimonides long ago stated that *sedaka*"—he used the mideastern pronunciation of *tsedaka*—"charity, is a prime virtue . . . Come, I will show you something. Do you want to see the synagogue?"

"Haven't I just seen it?"

The rabbi smiled. There was a green tinge of victory in his eyes. He knew something I did not know. He put his hand around my waist and gently steered me out into the hall.

"Dom Domingo," the rabbi called and said something to him in the native language. It was not Slavic, not Italian, not Arabic—but it had the sounds, and music, of all three tongues. Then he turned to me and said, "We are going upstairs."

Dom Domingo ran ahead, turning on lights. His wooden heels clicked and echoed in the long marble hall. The rabbi guided me to the carpeted red marble steps. As we walked up, I lifted the hem of my purple robe, held my crown straight so that it would not fall.

The rabbi pushed open two hand-carved oaken doors. They moved outward slowly, on silent hinges. Where a packed congregation was waiting for me to walk up to the bimah and deliver the royal address.

"There," the rabbi said, again that victorious glint in his eyes. "I saw your shivering down below. See? Lovely, eh? What do you think of this?"

Dom Domingo once again ran ahead, switching on all the lamps on the walls.

I looked up to the high ceilings, to the huge blue dome, painted with birds and stars, and at the stained glass windows, the pews, and the Ark. I looked up at the tiers, two—three—of balconies, with hand-carved friezes.

"Magnificent," I said. "I've never seen anything like this before . . . Why isn't this beautiful, even palatial, synagogue listed in the Jewish travel guides?"

"Well," he said. "Correspondence, letters, forms to fill. You know . . ."

"Do you ever use it?"

"For the holidays, if there are worshipers."

Dom Domingo snapped his fingers, pointed to the chairs on the bimah, ran his hand over the plush blue velvet and the gold trim.

"Dom Domingo never speaks in this synagogue," the rabbi whispered. "He is in awe of its beauty. I am sure there is a Jew floating somewhere in him. Why else would he have wanted to learn to read the Siddur?"

Dom Domingo pulled the curtain and opened the Ark. The beautiful old Torahs were lit up; old silver crowns, pointers, breast plates. Torahs encased in wooden containers, Torahs garbed in velvet.

The huge room was bathed in light, in contrast to the baroque cell below.

"Rabbi, from my letters—"

He lowered his head, looked contrite, as though to say: that is beyond me, letter-writing: forgive me.

"—you probably realize what I am looking for. Perhaps you can help me."

Once again Rabbi Gagliatacozzo put his arm around me, and steered me back toward the door.

Behind us Dom Domingo was turning off the lights. Gradually the room grew darker.

"What sort of archival material do you have here? Any old synagogue records? Or family histories?"

The rabbi placed his hand on my shoulder. "Forgive me for interrupting, but the four Harrera women can give you all the information you need. Their family has been here for centuries, and they have an extensive collection. Their father, Shlomo Harrera, was the president of the *kehilla* and keeper of the archives for fifty-five years. Once there was a time when Moorish, Christian, and Jewish scholars would congregate here. Mustara is still a place where the three cultures blend. But oh how times have changed! From the scholars of the past we now have ignoramuses who do not know how to read one Hebrew letter."

"The current president?"

The rabbi nodded. "A good man. You see he tries. But knowledge—nil."

"Do you think the women would let me see their collection?"

The rabbi folded his hands. "I cannot speak for the Harreras. Approach them directly."

"Perhaps tomorrow morning after services," I suggested.

"No, no. We do not have Shabbat morning services. Everyone works so we have no minyan. But the Harreras go to the Jewish Museum to pay their respect to the martyrs exhibit every Saturday. You can meet them there perhaps."

"Is anything from their collection on view at the museum?"

The rabbi lifted a finger, opened his mouth and said, "Ah . . . That is a question."

I waited for him to continue. The rabbi was a short man, dark like all the other people in Mustara, with a little mustache but no beard. He came from an old Italian family that, as articles on his distinguished forebears in various encyclopedias indicated, had moved here a century ago. Like all short men, he carried himself erectly, shoulders squared and neck stiff, to make himself appear taller. He wagged a finger at me, as though I were a naughty boy.

"There is a Hebrew proverb: a guest for a while sees for a mile."

It's a Yiddish proverb, not a Hebrew one, I wanted to remind him. The Ashkenazic Jews who fled persecutions in Central Europe probably brought it here in the 1870s.

"You see," Rabbi Gagliatacozzo continued, "until recently they have not given anything of their private collection to the Jewish Museum, although I am sure their father, the *kehilla* president, had intended to. But since old Harerra left no will—he died suddenly—the women keep it for themselves. But three weeks ago— perhaps their consciences plagued them—they finally lent some of their collection for display at the Jewish Museum."

I leaped forward and seized the rabbi's arm. "Anything by Yehuda Halevi?"

"You are hurting me," he said.

I apologized. He rubbed his arm slyly. "I believe so. In fact, the exhibition just closed," he said. His voice sounded morose, but a cruel gleam shone in his eyes.

"Why didn't you write me?" I whined. I was furious but tried to control my feelings. "You knew I was doing research on Yehuda Halevi. I told you that three times. How long does it take to write a letter?"

He put his hand on his heart. "Believe me, I didn't know he was so important to you. And it is very difficult for me to write. You understand."

He was hinting at the political situation; but I knew that correspondence went on unimpeded.

"Yehuda Halevi is my entire focus. My life's work. For years I've been studying his songs and poetry. Why didn't you let me know? I would have come a month earlier."

The rabbi looked at his watch. "The museum is closed now. They open at ten tomorrow. Perhaps you will find some pieces still out. They do not pack so quickly there. The attendant is not known for his zeal for work."

What could I do now? Cry? I was too old for that. Rage? Against whom? I was a stranger here and could not vent my frustration at will. I had come this far. It would be foolish to give up now just because I was peeved.

The rabbi looked at my face. I tried to mime anger into grief.

"I'm sorry. I didn't know he was so important to you," Rabbi Gagliatacozzo repeated. "In your letters—"

"In my letters I only told you of scholarly interest. But there is also a personal story."

The rabbi looked at his watch. Late for dinner, I thought. He's already sniffing the cholent or the stuffed corudas or whatever it is that he fills his paunch with on Friday night. Tough, I thought. Just *because* you're in such a rush, I'll play dumb and keep you longer.

"Would you like to hear it?"

"Of course I would. Tell me," the rabbi said.

"I really appreciate this opportunity to exchange words with a scion of such distinguished lineage," I told him in florid Hebrew. "You see, Yehuda Halevi means a lot to me. When I was a youngster I wasn't interested in things Jewish. I went through the usual route, Hebrew school, Bar Mitzva. It's a long story. I could take hours to tell you all the details, spin you a tale as complicated and fragile as a spider's web. In high school I was attracted to Donne, Blake—yes, the religious ones, *davke* the mystics—and began to write poetry. Later, in college, thanks to my roommate, I discovered Hebrew. And from Hebrew the path led to Israel and Zionism. I now had a sense of history, a place in the world. During the Holocaust the Germans murdered one-third of our people, but we still had something to hold on to. I began devouring the medieval Hebrew poets, especially Yehuda Halevi. Agreed with his sense of destiny for the Jewish people. Marveled at his eleventh-century nationalism, his courage, despaired at the silence that greeted him. But what fixed the link between me and him was that one day—would you like to hear more, Rabbi, or am I keeping you?"

"No. No. Please continue." I was amazed at his self-control; he did not shift his weight from foot to foot, gave no hint his eyes were straining for his watch.

"One day while in the library and thumbing through some old mid-nineteenth-century English translations of Spanish Golden Age Jewish poets, I came across four lines of a poem that shook me. I read them and trembled:

Stranger am I and pilgrim on this earth;
Only beneath the sod my heritage.
So far my youthful days have had *their* will
Ah, when shall I myself have *my* will?"

96

The rabbi was unmoved.

"You don't appreciate poetry?" I asked.

"On the contrary. I do. But what is so remarkable about these lines?"

"I admit they are youthful. Perhaps I wouldn't write like that now. Yehuda Halevi wrote this poem before he was twenty. But the stirring thing is this: these lines were word for word in a short poem *I* had written when I was a senior in high school. Before I'd ever heard of Yehuda Halevi or read him in translation. This meant that Yehuda Halevi and I had had the same thoughts. Thousands of miles away and hundreds of years apart, but our minds were locked. It's almost as if I were an extension of him. Isn't that something? Tell me," I said before he had a chance to answer, "have you ever been to Israel?"

"No."

"Wouldn't you like to go?"

"Of course. I mean to visit."

"Well?"

"I cannot." He looked around although we were alone. "The regime. My position here. It is difficult. The government does not recognize Israel. But still we must give thanks to God. The state preaches no religion—even a mild atheism, in fact—yet it lets all religions flourish. Even though it does not recognize Israel, Israeli tourists come and there is trade. Jews and Muslims here live side by side in peace. When the Germans came and brought their friend, Death, it was Muslims who saved Jewish children, and hid the Codex. So you see I cannot complain. Just compare us with other states. You know what I mean."

"All right. I just wanted to draw an analogy. Your whole training and upbringing has been love of Israel.

You've waited a lifetime and are finally permitted to go—but when the plane lands in Israel you are blindfolded and are shipped back."

"Why?"

"How should I know why?" The rabbi was beginning to irritate me. "It's only a story. Frustrating, right?"

"Certainly."

"Now you know how I feel. You want something so badly and then at the last minute it's taken away from you."

Dom Domingo approached; the rabbi ceased speaking. The shamash waited at the entrance.

Once again a wave of anger came over me. It circled and swooped like a vulture. It rose as I spoke to the rabbi, flapped wings, stared with bright red unblinking eyes, then descended heavily again. I was confused, resentful over wasted effort and wasted time. Blocked at the foot of my goal.

"It's a pity," the rabbi said gently.

"The day I arrive the exhibition closes. Change of place, change of luck, the Talmud says. I changed my place, but my luck—"

"Then I'm doubly at fault now." The rabbi clasped his hands. "I should have answered your letters."

Despite myself I felt sorry for him. "Never mind, Rabbi. I'll try to see what can be done."

He glanced over at Dom Domingo. "Come, the shamash wants to go home." The rabbi extended his hand. "Shabbat shalom. So, then, tomorrow at the Jewish Museum."

"Fine. What time will I see you there?"

"You misunderstand," the rabbi said. "*I* won't be there. *You* will."

"Well, then, may I call on you if I need more information?"

I expected him to say what rabbis and community leaders in Lisbon, Malaga, Naples, Malta, Dubrovnik, and Athens had said as I retraced Yehuda Halevi's footsteps and travels: Don't phone, come visit me at home.

But Rabbi Gagliatacozzo said: "Of course. I am in the local directory . . . Shabbat shalom!"

We stood at the threshold and shook hands.

I walked out of the synagogue and down the cobblestone lane. The rabbi walked slowly up the street. He looked tired, I thought. He tried to keep the Jewish community afloat but would do nothing to bring it to shore. True, his congregation was not inspiring, but still—I stopped. What was I doing? How could I judge a man until I was in his place? In a land where religion was officially discouraged, it was a miracle that synagogues were still standing. In other such countries, synagogues had been shut down, turned into warehouses, even dismantled. That Mustara had a Jewish museum too was a miracle. We have to seek out miracles where we find them, and once found, give thanks for their existence.

Across the street from the synagogue, I saw a man standing in a doorway, but I could not see him too clearly, for Synagogue Lane was not illuminated. Was he waiting for me? I hesitated, then said, "Shabbat shalom!" He stepped forward as if to cross the street toward me. The Harreras' cousin, Piadadé? What luck! Of all the people in the synagogue, he was the one I wanted most to meet. He lifted his hand in apparent greeting, then stopped, turned, and walked up the dark steep street. Did he want to speak to me but felt too shy? Or did he perhaps think he had no common tongue with me? Or was this whole encounter a creation of my imagination after having seen a man in a doorway and mistaking him for Piadadé?

I walked down the lane to the well-lit side street. I was not dressed warmly enough. Now the air had turned damp and cold, like January before a snowfall. Although it was past nine, most of the carts were still offering their wares for sale. Each peddler had his own boutique on wheels. Shirts and sweaters and scarves; pens, pencils, and wallets; trousers and jackets made out of cheap leather; unwrapped bars of soap; slips and brassieres. One cart sold an assortment of trinkets—miniature vases and pitchers decorated with native colors; another sold a nut indigenous only to the island; the seller weighed the nuts on a primitive brass scale remarkably like the one on the synagogue's mosaic floor. Couples and even grandparents with little children strolled through the streets in a holiday atmosphere, looking at the carts and touching the goods. From their faces one could not tell they were living in a land that limited freedom. But unlike people and towns deep in the East, their faces were not grey; the city was not somber.

Then an unheard whistle was blown. Obediently, the peddlers began to pack their stalls. The primitive wooden carts with wheels were rolled into a side alley and were not even locked up. All the wares were folded into large stiff, three-cornered canvas bags, and hoisted to their shoulders. Then, with backs bent, looking like huge runaway triangles, they walked home.

II

The Museum

The next morning, at 9:45, I was at the Jewish Museum. I walked past the wooden gate and stepped into a cobblestoned courtyard with a perfectly preserved Jewish quarter. Under a long shed with a sloped, tile-covered roof were a series of shops. The doors were open, as though the owners had just left to go for lunch and siesta at home and would soon return. The first was a shoemaker's shop. Cut leather was strewn about and an old boot was overturned on the last. Next was a cabinetmaker's stall with its smells of freshly sawn wood, varnish, and lacquer. From the large sand-colored stucco building on my right—the museum, formerly a synagogue—I heard rhythmic banging. Was the carpenter in there? I looked at my watch. Ten minutes to opening time. Nevertheless, I tried the door. Open. I stepped softly into a cool, unlit interior. My eyes adjusted. The walls were bare, but the photographs on exhibit, from the period before the German desecration of the sanctuary, showed that there had been elaborate Sephardic designs and Moorish-style decorations on the walls. While I wondered about the cessation of banging, it resumed. Heart beating, I ran to the noise at the far end of the ground floor. There, by the Ark, an attendant was hammering nails into a box. Two other locked boxes stood nearby.

STOP, I wanted to shout. But again I restrained myself. Such an incursion could only cause ill will. I eyed the treasure before me, and bit my tongue. I couldn't have been happier had I been permitted to see the Codex.

"Gra dnasta," I said.

"Gr' dnas," the attendant replied in the local dialect. He lay the hammer on the chest and stood. He was a tall handsome man with full face and curly hair, casually dressed—in a knit sportshirt with an open collar—as though he were a visitor to the museum and not its employee.

"Turistnak?" he asked.

"American," I replied.

"No speak Inglese. Small understand. Bissel Deutsch. Italiano. You speak Magyar? Russki? Portugese?"

"No," I said.

"Me nicht too. No Magyar, Russki, Portugese." He laughed broadly and shook my hand.

In the spirit of things, I asked: "Finnish? Ugaritic? Afrikaans?"

"No," he said. "Du?"

"Ich, no."

He laughed uproariously, as though hearing the joke for the first time. He wagged a finger in the air. "Norska no. Yugoslavaskem no. Japaniste no. Me nom sprech fifty lingua." He then took me from display to display on the ground floor. I listened to his mixture of broken German, Italian, Spanish, and English. That he knew no foreign languages did not faze him. He reinvented Esperanto. Unconcerned with grammar, he related his facts with authority and enthusiasm.

As he spoke, I kept glancing towards the entrance to see if the four women had come in. Perhaps they were upstairs already.

"Kooken, see. Bimah. Holy Ark." He knocked the wood. "Deutschen boom boom, chop chop. Reconstruzzione. No real. No echt," he said, tapping the replica of the Holy Ark and the wide, hand-carved, and crenellated bimah. Then he ran to a glass case in which hung the curtain—it looked like an old Persian carpet—to a Holy Ark. Deep crimson, with hand-stitched gold trimming motifs of the Torah, menorah, and Lions of Judah.

"But this echt, echt," he said enthusiastically. He pointed to his chest. "Me save from Deutschen. Me. In albergo till nach krieg."

I looked up at his beaming face.

"Kol Yisrael haverim," I told him.

He looked blankly at me.

"Yehudi?" I asked cautiously.

"No. Ich goy . . ."

"Christiano?"

He spat contemptuously and grimaced in distaste. "No. Me good goy. Muslim. Muslim. Muslim safe all. Muslim here Jude kinder von Deutschen avek albergo. Nicht lassen deutschen morto jude bambini. Niente."

Solemnly, I shook his hand, thanking his people for their deeds of kindness. It was true. He was echoing what I had heard and read. Indeed, the Muslims here had saved Jewish children; they had also saved the foremost Jewish treasure in the world, the oldest handwritten Hebrew codex of the Bible. They had done it at great personal risk, unselfishly, with no thought of reward.

Now was the time, I thought, to talk of the boxes. Now amenities had passed. We had spoken together, laughed together, recalled a tragic past together. Now was the time to speak of boxes, and of hammer and nails. But as I cleared my throat he was on his knees hammering again.

"Stop," I shouted. "Wait. Momento!"

The man stopped and turned to me. "Que cosa?"

I counted five nails in the chest.

"Exhibito?" I pointed to the chest.

"Sì."

"Yehuda Halevi?"

"Sì."

"Pay porud. Much." I rubbed my fingers. "Long travel. Mille kilometer. Comprende?"

"Sì."

"Accidente. Day late. Uno giorno. Mala fata."

The attendant made a "tsk-tsk" sound.

"Because rabbi no answer my letter."

The attendant waved his hand deprecatingly. "Rabbi no escrito. Niemals. Nicht gut. Rabbi essen, trinken, mangiare, dormo! Zzz!" He laughed.

"Go find keys. Schlissel. Open. Overto, per favore."

The attendant tapped his pockets as if looking for the keys. He ran to a little table and opened the drawer. He shrugged. "No keys. With signoras."

I made a pry-open motion with my fist. "Per favore."

"Impossibile," he said. "Non permeto."

"Permeto. Molto importante. Please, my life work. Vita. Vita o morte."

He shrugged "Me no can. Signoras . . ." he made a slitting motion on his throat.

"Tell me. Manuscritto originale? Yehuda Halevi?"

"Non lo so. Per favore," he pleaded. "Non lo so. Ich no professore. Sono simplissimo, signore. Ich idiotkem!"

Then to hammering again. I watched a sixth nail sink into the chest, a seventh. With each nail driven in, I felt my skin pierced, my flesh cut. My body was the wood, being closed, boxed in.

"Look. I'll pay you well. Porud."

He banged in another nail with a fury. "*You* look. Molto parlare, no see porud. You say, pay well, pay well. Mano in pocket. No money in mano. Empty. Like ausgesucked egg."

"I *pay,*" I insisted. I pointed to my heart, my mouth, to heaven above. "Promisi. At least one box open. How would they know you open again? Suppose—"

"Eh?"

"Imaginare . . . you no close box. It's like coming the day after the ship sailed. An hour after the train pulled out. When the soccer match has ended."

He did not understand my quick talk, but I sensed my words were making an effect, like music. Now he slowed the pace of his hammering, concentrated on what I was saying. The blood rose to his face. "So you will be helping me and you. And not hurting them. Just one day differenze! I came too late. Stop banging. Pry open."

I had an idea. He was a Muslim. They loved poetry. Imagery. Hyperbole. Exaggerated conceits. For them life was an extended metaphor. "One more nail and ich morto," I said. "Finito. Finished. Kaput You've just about killed me. Closed the lid on me. I'm dead. Morto. Finito."

The hammer stopped in mid-air. "All right. Show porud."

"I don't have any with me right now. Sabato. Saturday."

He grimaced, waved his hand at me like he'd done at the mention of the rabbi's letter-writing. And continued hammering.

"Samstag," I shouted. "Shabbes. Shabbat. Sabato. Giorno numero sette. I'll bring it to you tonight."

"You full bullsheet," he said, starting in on the last nail. "Signoras no permeto. Belong to them. If to museum, then differente story."

I resisted an impulse to fantasize violence. But dreamt of taking the hammer and splitting the chest open. Prying open the lids and removing vessels and manuscripts hundreds of years old. Or luring him to one of the workshops and locking him in while I closed the museum doors and inspected all the chests. For they had no right to deny me my material. Yehuda Halevi was mine. All this—whether authentic or junk— had no business being here in this offbeat island. It should have been in some accessible place, like New York or Jerusalem, where a museum would house it and scholars and people would enjoy it.

"Finito," the attendant said, banging down the last nail, and pushed the chest aside. He again made a helpless gesture and then suddenly broke into a smile and extended his hand. "Amigo," he said.

"Me finito. Morto."

What could I do? Perhaps it was good to have him as a friend. I took his hand. My only hope now was to see the Harreras. I still did not give up. Locked yes, lost no!

Now I wanted to wander about the museum by myself, but the attendant, bored that no one else was there, and guilty about refusing me, immediately volunteered—"me amigo tu"—to guide me upstairs too.

I waved no with my hands, "Grazia. Privato." He understood.

"When do you expect four women?" I asked.

"Prego?"

"Vier frauen." I raised four fingers and made a vague motion with my hands outlining the figure of a woman, American-style.

"Ah." He led me to the display case where I saw the manikin of a seventy-year-old Sephardic rabbi's wife, complete with ankle-length brocaded dress, mantilla, and heavy silver jewelry. It was dated 1863. "You like signorina?"

"Nein. Four living women. Madam. Signori. Quatro. When kommen? A que hora . . ." But I forgot the word for "arrive."

The attendant pulled a face of stupefaction. He lowered his lips and shrugged his shoulders. "Me told you. Ich idiotkem."

"It's okay," I said, waving him away. By the staircase I saw a short rounded tombstone with large Hebrew lettering that had been removed from the cemetery; but in order to keep its sanctity, it had been ensconced in soil. I looked at it, bowed my head, then walked up the stairs to what had once been the women's gallery.

I walked up one flight, two, three. I knew what to expect at the martyr's exhibit, but was not prepared for what I saw. Past the first arch I saw a huge red book, five feet long and two feet wide, suspended from the ceiling on a brass link chain. On the walls hung pictures, pictures of the dead, torn Torah scrolls, megillahs, and prayer shawls bullet-riddled and stained with blood. I hesitated, heart beating, before I opened the book. It swung heavily, lugubriously on the chain, like an overweight bell, but the chain did not creak. There was not a sound. No footfalls, no hammering, no breathing. Not a sound in the museum that had once been a synagogue, not a sound in the museum that had a tombstone with the name of a man long dead, and not a sound from the pictures of the dead artists and writers and leaders whose only tombstones were the works that had been saved from the pyre, and photographs on which even the living faces bore the shadow of death. The book swung slowly, like a clapper without a bell, a mute tongue looking for its bell.

The four women were not upstairs.

The sun came in from an arched window; it glinted on the twisted, gilded chain. Sparks flew. Sparks slid down a chain of fire of their own formation. I saw the faces of the children who lived only in photographs. I attempted to swallow. Could not. There was a taste of steel in my mouth. A large metal scoop dippled the soul out of me; I felt a hollowness where my heart had been.

I turned the huge pages of the red book. It contained a story which read:

Abramson
Abulafia
Ahuv
Azaga
Bendavid
Bergelson
Bezen
Cohen, David

Cohen, Mazal
Cohen, Beruriya

I turned a page, a slow, heavy, oppressive page.

Finzi, Giorgio
Friedmann, 🎵 Ferdinand א

The musical sign caught my eye, penetrated the memory. The aleph too.
I turned to the Ls.

Laban, Isak
Lapide
Lapidot

I looked for my name. Wherever there is a list of names, a petition, a phone book, a library catalogue, a book index, a periodical index, I look for my name. Who knows, perhaps I may find it? Where my name is, I am. There is my reality. Not seeing my name in a list would be as surprising to me as not seeing my image when I looked in a mirror. I looked for my name among my kinsmen.

Lev, Yosef
Levi, Janos
Levia, Gabriella
Leviant, Curt

I closed my eyes. In black print between Levia, Gabriella, and Leviatan, Arie. On textured off-white thick paper with flaking lint. Though my eyes were closed, the page was lit in my mind's eye as if a beacon from my brain were illuminating my name. I opened my eyes. Still, still there. My name was not gone. I had not erred. My name—I—was there.

Someone was climbing the stairs. I shut the book so that he would not see, held it still, and looked at a photographic display. One is still apologetic about death, even though one still walks the earth as if nothing happened.

The museum attendant came up, looked suspiciously at me for a moment, and then, embarrassed, straightened a frame which was perfectly centered on the wall. I realized my hands were in my pockets. I pulled them out as if to say: see, my hands are clean. I have taken nothing.

I had an idea. "Tell me." I opened the book to the page with Fs.

"Tell me, porque namen Friedmann con musica. Drei noten?"

"Ah, Friedmann!" He brightened. "Cantore. Grosse canto. Ein mentch mucho bellissimo gesingen tra la-la-la. Musica." He kissed his fingers. "In sinagoga singen like angelos. . . . But Deutschen him morto. Finito. Friedmann bel cantore, il poverito!"

"And why the *aleph,* first letter, prima lettera of Hebrew alphabet?"

He gave that helpless shrug again. "Me no know."

Later, I heard him climbing the stairs again, more slowly, as though he were giving me fair warning to return the things I'd taken. I was going to tell him I didn't appreciate his spying on me.

"Shabbat shalom."

"Shabbat shalom!" I said, surprised. "Rabbi, I thought you were not going to come here."

He raised a finger. "You were distressed yesterday, so I came to—After all, you are a stranger here, in a strange land, and we are bidden to help the stranger"—he used the evocative Biblical phrase—"I want to see if I can help you."

"Very kind of you. I came early, per your instruction, but I got no cooperation."

"I know. Yussuf told me downstairs. He can do nothing. Museum property would be another matter. I could have a voice there. But it belongs to the Harreras. Private property. With them it is not so simple."

I almost told him about the bribe, but decided not to endanger Yussuf's job. Yussuf, in any case, would deny it, and I'd be held in suspicion. Who knows what fines, imprisonment, a bribe would bring? A crime against the State.

The rabbi glanced at the large red book, then lowered his eyes. "Tell me, how did you come here? What led you to Mustara?"

"As I told you yesterday, it's my interest in Yehuda Halevi. I've read everything by and about him. Spent years tracking down hundreds of leads from sources you've never dreamt of. Studied inscriptions on buildings, community records, obscure philosophical tracts. One hint led me to another. Do you know Donatello Ferrari?"

"I've heard of him. His books are not easily accessible here. The Gagliatacozzo family stems from Ferrara, you know. Our tree lists Donatello as an ancestor."

"Donatello Ferrari, master of Hebrew eros. What poems! In several of his bawdy bilingual lyrics he refers to Yehuda Halevi as 'en Maestro,' or 'en Maestru,' which is an enigmatic substitution of preposition for article. This puzzled me, until while scanning one of Yehuda Halevi's minor poems, I found that the name Mustara had been interwoven like an acrostic into the opening verses of the poem. Now I understood the pun—"

"En Maestru—in Mustara," the rabbi said excitedly.

"Exactly! And then there was the chance remark of another Halevi contemporary, that neglected Muslim thinker from Toledo, Ibrahin Waqtal. He claimed that Halevi was not a doctor but a pharmacist, a dispenser of medicines rather than a practitioner. And besides, there were varied suggestions that Yehuda Halevi had also been an illuminator of manuscripts, a side of the poet-philosopher hitherto unknown."

"And that is why you came here."

"Yes. I'm not a two-hour tourist, as you so aptly put it. I came to see what traces the Sweet Singer of Zion had left here for me."

"For you?"

"Yes. For me. I say it purposely. We wrote the same poem. He knows me."

"Evidently not well enough." The rabbi smiled slyly.

"Perhaps . . . On the day that I arrived the exhibition closes."

"Yes, you told me that yesterday." Then, obviously to change the subject, he added, "Have you seen the Harreras yet?"

"No, I'm waiting for them."

"Then all is not lost. Wait. They will surely come. They'll listen to reason."

"I hope so." Then added, "Three boxes, and all locked. It's incredible."

"It's incredible that lazy Yussuf did the job so quickly . . . What do you think of our museum?"

"Museums are magnificent institutions."

The rabbi stuck out his hand. "Well, I'm glad I was able to help you. The bazaar, you know, is just a few steps away, and since it is Shabbat, there is no temptation to buy. Who knows, you may even find something you are looking for."

Rabbi Gagliatacozzo walked down the stairs. Then I heard him walking back up. He'd changed his mind. Just as he had come to the museum because he felt guilty about rebuffing me, he was now returning to invite me—who had not yet been shown traditional Jewish hospitality—to a Shabbat lunch.

But it was Yussuf again. He took a key, unlocked a glass cabinet displaying books published just before the war, removed a feather duster from his back pocket, and dusted the books. Then he cleared his throat. "Is signor lost? Help needed?"

"No, no," I said. "Atmosphere absorbing. Inbreathing effects metaphysical. Spiration philosophical."

"Ach ja," he nodded. "Philosophia. Spiration."

Just then, through the arched window, the highest window in the museum, I saw the four women—how small they looked from here—walking on the sidewalk below—*away* from the museum.

"Quatra signorina? Da? Here? Gekommen? Entrata aqui?" I asked.

Yussuf pulled the stupid face of before.

"Those four Harreras," I said, pointing to the window. He craned his neck, but by the time he looked the four had already gone out of sight. I wanted to run down the stairs.

"Que quatra signorina? Nicht sehen. No comprendo."

Yussuf beckoned to the case he had opened and asked me to step toward it. He winked conspiratorially—my heart quickened. I thought he had something for me.

"Momento. Interesante. Questione."

Yussuf looked to see if anyone was around. "Tell me," he whispered. "What . . . que . . ." and made a churning motion with both hands. "Spiration?"

I took a deep breath for him, illustrating. "Inspiration, aspiration, conspiration," then let it out with a sigh. "Suspiration . . . expiration."

And then three at a time, I spiraled down the turning stairs. I stopped short at the entrance to the museum, breaking my own momentum and looking to each side for the four Harrera women. Nowhere in sight.

I turned right, followed the crowds through the narrow lane, twining through the twisting alleyways tight with noisy shoppers and peddlers until I suddenly came to a large, open square lined with booths on three sides and a mosque on the other. A huge minaret penciled above me. Thousands of white pigeons covered the square like fleece. A child ran into them, and the cover of pigeons billowed up in almost perfect saucer shape, then descended. At the periphery crouched a kerchiefed peasant woman in a colorful costume; she threw seeds to the pigeons. Tourists with cameras were taking pictures. It was such a tranquil scene that even the grey, jagged mountain peaks seemed less foreboding.

I am alive, I thought. Even though I had seen my name in that book of ashes. I am alive; I see white pigeons breathing like a blanket of snow. In me there is a pillar of fire. I am alive. I want. Dead men do not want. I have memory. I remember writing a poem that Yehuda Halevi must have dictated to me. I wanted those four women to lead me to, to unlock for me, the lost past I treasured.

I wandered through the marketplace. The stalls sold cheap hand-woven rugs in garish colors, wooden trays and bowls, copper cooking utensils. Each lane had its own color, smells, and specialty. The copper lane, with extended tin roofs that looked like metallic trees joining, glowed orange-red, and the tang of solder hung in the air. Nearby was baker's row; the heat flowed past with scent of freshly baked rolls. Bakers' assistants ran in and out of shops carrying trays of bread on their heads. Then, suddenly, the fruit market. One woman sold only cherry-sized shiny yellow plums. She sat on a chair, and quart-size baskets of the gleaming fruit surrounded her. Another woman sold purple figs. Here cherries were sold; there apricots, strawberries, melons of all kinds, peaches, and fruits I had never seen before. Hands flew in cacophony, weighing—here too they used scales like that on the mosaic floor—wrapping, spinning paper bags to close them. Samples were offered cheerfully. No one left the market hungry. I turned into a lane where handcrafted silver necklaces and trays were on display. In one little shop I noticed a chain with a design that looked like a Star of David. Although I had no money with me, I entered the small shop, which could accommodate no more than three people.

The owner was repairing a silver chain when I walked in. He stood, a small bald man with a lined oval face and dark, deep-set, bespectacled eyes. A Jew, I realized. One of the members of the congregation who does not come to Sabbath services.

"You speak English?"

"A little, sir."

"How much is the Magen David in window?"

I expected his eyes to light up, a smile to infuse his face, as one of the code words was recited.

"Pardon?" he said.

"The Magen David."

He blinked. "Pardon! I do not understand."

A Marrano perhaps. Afraid. Europe, but still Muslim. West-appearing, but still East.

"This," I said, and went to the showcase.

"Oh. Fine craftsmanship. Twenty years old. Made by little girl, sir. You see? Fine work, little fingers. Look at tiny links. All handiwork. Feel weight." He moved his hands up and down, then gave the chain to me. "Feel weight? Made by Sahali tribe, way up in mountains above Mustara, near the peaks of snow. Note design, sir." He pushed his glasses up to his forehead. For the first time I noticed the black, argent-stained edges of his fingers.

"Do you sell coins?" I asked.

"Yes, yes," he replied in that soft, sure, professorial voice of his. He pulled out a key and unlocked a cabinet door below the counter, and lifted out a tray of coins. I sifted through the patinaed coins.

"I am looking for old Spanish coins. Twelfth century."

He rubbed his chin with thumb and index-finger and squeezed his lips. "No. They are hard to find. Not my spetzialitet. Spanish coins here are very rare."

"But Spanish Judeo settle here," I protested. "They bring old coins with them."

He raised a finger as though to say: you have a point. "You are right. Try Harreras. Old Spanish Judeo family. Perhaps they have old coins. They have good collection of everything." He lifted the silver necklace. "You still want this?"

"How much?"

"Eighty porud."

"Too much."

"You are tourist? For tourist, spetzial rate."

"Me scholar passing through."

"Then for passing scholar seventy."

"Look, I have no money today. Can I buy tomorrow?"

"Sunday we are closed. Sunday no business for me."

"Perhaps we arrange privately?"

"Cannot. Government say close shops. Shops must be closed. Tsk, tsk," he said. "Cannot do. Why not Monday?"

"Me Monday in library all day," I said. "Cannot."

"What is library?"

"Bibliotek."

"Cannot do. All shops closed. Quiet in bazaar. Like in library," he laughed. "I give it for sixty-five porud."

"No money today, Thank you." I left the store and began looking into other silver shop windows.

He followed me outside. "If no money today, then I sell for sixty."

I still don't know if he was joking.

III

The Bazaar

The next day I wanted to see the other sections of Mustara, but I was drawn like a magnet to the bazaar. Everything was indeed closed. A bell rang, muffled, distant, from a lone church in the Christian quarter. A muezzin called morning prayers from a minaret. In the clear, still air his wavering halftones rang like a Sephardic melody. My heels clacked and echoed. I looked up at saw-edged mountain tops, the ice peaks glinting like slivers of broken glass. The sun lay flat on the roofs of the low-lying shacks, roofs huddling under deep matte red tiles, gracefully rounded, as fresh as the day they were placed. The white pigeons hovered in the broad empty square. Gone the pigeon lady. The pigeons pecked at shadows, yesterday's figment of their white imagination. They cooed in groups, rose and fluttered and settled down. I walked through the market—ghost stalls, empty lanes—retracing yesterday's path until I found the little shop. Inside, a woman nodded, inviting me in.

Yesterday, in the crush of the bazaar, the shop had seemed narrow; today it was even smaller, oppressively so, hardly larger than a newsstand. Walls decorated with bronze and copper plates and pitchers and silver chains, pendants, brooches. A feather whisk broom hung on the wall like an objet d'art. Today I noticed things I missed yesterday.

"Gra dnasta," I said.

"Dnasta gra," she replied in the literary style, with a tilt of her head and a welcoming smile. The poetic turn of her greeting had a tone that was at once distinguished, intimate, and mocking. *"Gra dnasta nird dogla ped."*

"I'm sorry. I speak English."

"We close today. Excuse," she said, passing her hand over her hair and one silver earring. "I no speak English good."

"I know you close today. That's what the man here—your husband?—told me yesterday. That's why I'm here."

I shut the door behind me.

"Offitzially we close," she said. But the warmth of her voice belied her words. She walked around the counter, squeezing behind me. "Excuse," she said, but did not turn to the wall as another woman might have done out of modesty. Instead, she pressed her back against the wall and rubbed her breasts into my back. What if I had turned to her? My back to the counter and her back to the wall as she pressed by me? She lingered by the door for a moment.

As she stood testing the handle, I noticed for the first time that she was much younger than her husband—if indeed he was her husband and not her father. She too had an oval olive face and deep-set black eyes. Her smooth skin and fine straight nose gave her face insouciance and maturity. She stood straight and tall, while her husband (father?) reminded me of an owlish watchmaker with a magnifying glass pressed into his eye, hunched over, inspecting the insides of a watch. She turned her head, bared her long neck. Her silver earrings, laced with serpents, wavered.

"Yes? You interested in something?"

I was perspiring. It was warm in the little shop, and though near noon, a dusky copper light pervaded. She was thirty or thirty-three and her breasts were firm and ample. They punched two little holes of desire into my back. I was enchanted by the copper light, by the erotic crescence of her earrings, by the postcoital glow of her face. Time seemed to stop for me, as it did the other night in the synagogue. I relaxed in the tight Sunday light and warmth of the little shop. I closed my eyes for a moment. Lines from Donatello Ferrari's sexually charged lyrics flashed before me. I daydreamt I was swimming underwater with her, tumbling and turning, we eluding one another with swift fins, like fish the nets. A sweet heat exuded—from the room? From me? I was in a strange country, a strange culture, but the moist scent of hair, perfume, and perspiration—flowers and salt mingled—was the same, remarkably the same: a woman in heat!

I opened my eyes, saw a small blue porcelain pitcher floating past the doorway just above the woman's head. The pitcher stopped. I saw a being with two heads and four hands, topped by a blue porcelain pitcher.

"You see something?" the woman asked. She leaned against the glass door as though protecting herself against a potential violator.

"A blue porcelain pitcher and a man holding a blue porcelain pitcher."

As the man knocked, the woman turned. He said something to her in the native language. She shook her head, shrugged her shoulders, and whispered harshly.

He spoke louder and pointed to the pitcher. I watched his hands, and held my breath.

"Beautiful," I exclaimed, approaching the door. I pressed my nose to the glass, while the woman stood next to me, her shoulders touching mine, as if acknowledging the remark she assumed I had addressed to her. I focused my eyes on the sky-blue, gracefully rounded little pitcher, and my shoulder on the woman's supple arm. Perhaps her husband would come and see me pressed up against his wife and wonder why I was locked into his little shop with her while yet another man stood outside begging to get in.

The man turned and spoke to me, but I did not understand him. The woman stepped back, as if retreating from him, but when he began to point at the lines written on the pitcher, the woman leaned closer and pressed her body into mine. If thoughts were passports I would have been the sultan. Instead, I concentrated on the pitcher. I saw Hebrew letters there but in my state of excitation I saw Hebrew everywhere, even in the formation of the stars. Candelabras became menorahs, and hexagons signaled private messages out of a distant past.

"What is he say?" she asked.

I turned my head. "But you should know. It's your language he's speaking."

She smiled. First time I saw her smiling. I looked for blemishes on her oval complexion, some puffiness, a few blackheads, an excuse to forget her presence. But her face was surprisingly clear and smooth, her teeth even and white. From her hair came that scent of perfume and spices that floated over the tiny room.

"Does he want to sell the pitcher?" I asked.

"Yes, but today Sunday that we are offitzially close."

Now she smiled when she said this, and lifted one shoulder provocatively.

"A woman is offitzially closed too until the right key comes to open the lock," I said. "Open the door and we can all talk privately."

I thought she would hesitate, but she quickly moved away from me and opened the door. The man came in clutching his unbuttoned thin blue coat. He had a creased face and a three-day growth of beard that gave a tragic cast to his sad, hooded eyes. In New York I would have called him a man who had lost all hope. But here many people looked like this—was it genes, that special blend of East and West, Islam and the cross? Yet, despite frayed clothing, a coat with baggy pockets, grey trousers, and dark blue jacket so shiny in spots it reflected duskily the porcelain pitcher he carried, he still retained his dignity. When he looked me full in the face, I saw a glimmer of recognition. I flipped cards in my mind. The bus ride up from the port city of Kal'ir? The Pension Royale? Then—of course! Friday night in the synagogue: Menahem Piadadé. Estranged cousin to the four Harreras.

"Shalom," I said.

He looked at me to see if I had used the word mockingly. "Shalom," I repeated.

"Shalom," he replied, still unsure, in a slightly rasping voice. He set the pitcher on the counter, but did not remove his hand from it.

"May I see it?" I asked in Hebrew.

"Careful," he said in a low voice, still clasping the handle even as I held it. He pulled a cloth bag from his coat pocket. "This is a precious vessel."

He used an old Hebrew word for "vessel," which showed me he knew the language well.

"Where did you learn Hebrew?"

"Here. During my childhood." He leaned toward me and, in a tone of helpless defeat, shyly added, as though baring his vulnerability, "Before the enemy came we all knew Hebrew here."

Did he mean the Germans, or the totalitarian regime that followed?

I held the pitcher and ran my hand over it gently, feeling its contours and the raised paint like embossed print. Sensing our rapport, the woman now quickly went behind the counter. Her eyes flashed. She said something to Piadadé, but the man shook his head. Although she leaned close to him, the womanly scent now was gone.

She unlocked a drawer and waved some paper *porud* notes.

"*Nej! Nej!*" Piadadé shook his head.

Meanwhile, I inspected the pitcher, spun it slowly in my hand, looked at the lines until I felt the dark-blue letters on the azure porcelain. At the edges of the tiny Hebrew lines, green-stemmed red roses and blue irises intertwined in a Shah Abbas Persian carpet design. But I saw more than words. Tucked in between the flowers and the tendrils, dotted with yellow sunflowers and lemons, were pictures of a pharmacist's shop, a judge holding a scale, a crowd of people apparently watching the judge. Some were wearing high cylindrical hats, the heads of others were covered with hoods. And then I discovered another picture; it was so small, it seemed that the artist had wanted to conceal it: a portrait of a man drinking so deeply from a bowl his head was almost out of view. Also, from the lemon branches dangled a pitcher that looked very much like the pitcher I was holding. Perhaps in that tiny pitcher was another picture of a man holding a pitcher and so on through the mirrors of infinity until the atoms of pitcherhood were seen.

The azure blue porcelain had a splendid translucency. It was a work of art, a rare antique. The writing was precise and clear, done by an excellent miniaturist hand, but it was too small to be read at first glance. A porcelain illuminated manuscript. I had never seen anything so lovely before. There are times when an object takes possession of you before you take possession of it, and nothing matters, not price, not inconvenience, until you possess that thing which possessed you first. My eyes unfocused momentarily. I slid into vertigo, swung on a swing with eyes shut tight. I minisculed into the pitcher. The water rose above my face. I gasped for breath. The woman's firm hands brought me back: The pitcher! I imagined Piadadé walking away with it. I could not bear the thought. I wanted that pitcher. I coveted that pitcher.

"I'll buy it from you," I told Piadadé in Hebrew. "Don't take her offer."

"I know what you say," the woman shouted at me. She wagged her finger coquettishly. Her earrings moved. "I don't understand your words, but I know what you do." But then the color of her face changed. Suddenly she swooped forward to grab the pitcher. The man spun like a wheel, quick as a whip—I had not thought he could move so swiftly—deflected her fingers, but his hands seized air. I saw the precious blue vessel floating slowly to crash to the floor. I sank down—

"Elohim, Elohim," Piadadé keened.

—and spread my arms—

"Idiotkem," he shouted at the woman.

But cradled in my hands, the pitcher was safe. I rose and presented it to Menahem Piadadé. He embraced me; his unshaven prickly face scratched mine.

"Ay ay," he said. "Ay ay."

But I know there was no thanks due me, for I had not acted altruistically; I had only saved what was mine.

"And I wanted to talk to you Friday night," Piadadé said, "but I—"

"Come outside," I told him. "She doesn't want to do business on Sunday."

He put the pitcher into the cloth bag and placed it deep in his coat pocket.

The woman, contrite now, was near tears. She tried to charm him, in the native language I could not understand. Then to me she said, "And I open up my store espetzially for you. Even though today Sunday. You know what government like here. To breaking law can make unpleasant for me. But if you close door on other side of him I show you things you like."

The magnetic needle in me faced two north fields: pitcher and woman, two facets of the same desire. Two holy vessels, as Donatello Ferrari called them in one of his poems.

Piadadé stepped out of the door. My legs followed my will outside. I wavered on the threshold.

"I give him big loan for it," the woman said.

"She's offering you a small loan," I whispered in Hebrew. "Don't take it."

Piadadé shook his head. "No. I must sell it for cash. It's a matter of rent."

"Do you really want to sell this beautiful pitcher?"

"I need money for rent."

"Then I'll buy it from you. And you'll have money for your rent."

"But then I won't have the pitcher."

I checked my impatience. You are not in the West, I told myself. The woman came around that little counter, walked quickly—no more than three strides—to the door. Once more she pressed up against me, one hand on my shoulder. "Don't go," she said. "I open my store spetzial for you."

"I'll be back," I promised.

I stepped outside.

"Fifty porud," Piadadé said. His eyes scanned the dead market, silent as Sunday.

Fifty! I thought he would ask one hundred fifty. But even that would have been a bargain. But I did not want to make the purchase so quickly. I remembered how Abraham had bargained with Ephron the Hittite for Sarah's burial plot. In the East one talks of other things first, one bargains indirectly, so as not to appear hasty or greedy.

"Where does this pitcher come from?"

"Come from? Come from?" he said hastily. He rubbed his pocket as if to say *that* was where it came from.

"How old is it? Has it been in your family for many years?"

Piadadé did not reply. Perhaps he hadn't understood. He fingered the shiny lapel of his jacket. Not to call attention to it—but nevertheless the threads were visible.

"Are you a collector?" he asked.

"Not really. I am a hunter."

A sphere of fright glimmered in his eyes. "Hunter?"

"I hunt for old objects," I laughed. "To discover Yehuda Halevi. I want to re-create his time." Now I could wait no longer. There was a time to speak of boxes, of hammer and nails, a time to speak of cerulean pitchers.

"Do you want to sell?"

"Forty porud," Piadadé said in a dead voice.

"No, no," I said. "You misunderstand me. It's worth much more. I'll give you one hundred . . . one hundred ten, even one hundred fifteen."

His sad, mourning eyes lit up for a moment. My offer had startled him. He had expected me to bargain. After all, we were in the bazaar, and though the majority in the country were Christians, the Muslim influence in Mustara was strong.

I took Piadadé by the arm and walked down a deserted alley in the bazaar. Shops on both sides were closed. A lone white pigeon cooed down at us from a slanted tiled roof. I saw the jagged dark mountain peaks that oppressed Mustara, but I closed my eyes to them. I took the money out of my pocket.

As Piadadé's hand went into his pocket, a light—the little light left there—went out in his eyes. Seeing how difficult it was for him to part with the pitcher, I asked, "Family heritage?" I assumed he would understand these oft-used Hebrew words.

Piadadé gave a half-nod, but said nothing. He looked morose, as though his soul were drifting out of him. I was sorry I did not offer him one hundred twenty-five porud. After all, what was a ten-porud note to me? To him very likely a month's rent. On the other hand, perhaps the man felt insulted. A proud man, he did not want charity.

We stood in the silent stasis of the Sunday marketplace. Nothing moved. No roof tile cracked, no pigeon cooed, croo croo. Little shops crowded in. Copper and silver cases and vessels pressed the windows. I felt I was floating through a motion picture. On the screen behind me chromatic scenes shifted, right out of a travelogue. I looked down at the rough grainy surface of the roof tiles, fascinated by the arched shadows. The cobblestones so high, they grew like grass. No walkers in the Sunday bazaar.

Soon Piadadé would have no pitcher. Perhaps the pitcher had been in his family for generations. Thousands of hours of watching, and possession had not removed any of its essence. Yet now he has exchanged it for money that would soon be gone. Money and love—*mortale,* Ferrari sang in one of his rare Italian verses, but a work of art—*eternale.*

To spur some conversation, I asked, "What can you use this pitcher for?"

Piadadé did not reply. He pulled the bag out of his pocket, looked longingly at it as though he regretted the sale. "Here. But do not open it until you get home. Sunday. Eyes are watching everywhere. Even in the dead bazaar."

As soon as I held the pitcher I felt my hands stretching it back to him. I felt sorry for him. A troubled man. He had come to services, but did not pray. At the very first sounds of the Sabbath hymn, "Come my beloved to greet the bride," he had disappeared. Perhaps I should give it back to him. But how can I give him something that had always been mine? Wasn't it destined that I meet Piadadé in the deserted marketplace? A native of the city, he knew well enough that on Sunday shops were closed; still he had come. To bring me my porcelain pitcher, with its Hebrew lines and illuminations.

Piadadé did not answer me. I repeated the question in my mind, weighed its timbre, its implications;

wondered if the words could have another meaning. What can you use this pitcher for? Yes, I realized, it could also have meant: What good was the pitcher? As though casting an aspersion on such a precious vessel. I rephrased the question, and Piadadé immediately said:

"Perhaps it can open up doors."

I heard myself repeating these words, whether out loud or in my mind's ear, I do not recall. Did I want to hear mystery in his voice, infuse Kabbala into his eyes?

Piadadé looked up and down the market street. "Please give me the money."

I apologized. "I didn't want to delay you. Do you have change of a hundred porud? I only have two hundred-porud notes in my pocket."

"I must go home. I'm cold. It's late."

"The woman will give us change. Come."

We returned to her shop. Crowded, enveloped, with people. Through the window I recognized the Harreras.

"The four women," I exclaimed.

Piadadé turned, froze, and broke away.

"Wait!" I shouted. "The money!"

Piadadé ran as though a demon were racing after him. I placed the pitcher in my jacket, and burst into a gallop. The earth pedaled away from me. Stores whizzed past. Copper vessels a blur. I was flying, a white pigeon giving chase. Piadadé was swift on his feet. His coat billowed behind him. I turned corners like a cat. Shouted: "Wait! Your money!" But I couldn't shout and run at the same time. He knew the alleys and lanes. I lost sight of him. Piadadé disappeared. Hiding or gone. Was the antipathy between him and the four women so great that they could not bear one another's presence? I stopped. How could I give him the money?

The rabbi. The sisters. No, of course not. My God! The sisters! I was wasting precious time. I ran back to the shop. The pigeons stared down at me from the roofs. Who was flying—they or I?

As I approached, I saw the four women outside, hunched forward, hawklike, their heads turning left and right, proceeding in a swift hunt. To the swiftest goes the chase. Were they like me, hunters for objects of the past? They peered into each store window, hands to their foreheads, looking in at the displays. Didn't they know that on Sundays the market was shut down tight?

Then they re-entered the little shop and examined some items on the counter.

The shopkeeper smiled as I walked in, as though she had won a victory. "You come back to Roza."

"I told you I'd be back."

"Gra dnasta," I told the Harreras. "Shalom!"

Only one of them replied, *"Gra dnasta."*

Now I had them. Now they could not escape.

"I've been looking for you. Travelled thousands of miles to see you. The rabbi told me about your distinguished family and your magnificent archives."

"Call at home," said the woman who appeared to be the mother or the eldest sister. Her head trembled as she spoke, as if she were shaking "no no no." "Regrets," she said. "No time now."

"Tuesday afternoon. At home," said her sister.

"But I don't even know where you live . . . The rabbi . . ."

"Perfect," said another sister, "The rabbi will tell you. Now we are looking . . ."

"For something important," the eldest continued. "We must go now."

I blocked their path.

"Just one more question. When can you open the boxes in the museum for me? I came too late, Yehuda Halevi is my life's work."

The eldest Harrera bent forward, he head swaying back and forth quickly. She fixed her blue-eyed gaze at me. "Do you know Yehuda Halevi?"

My heart surged. I'd gotten a response from her.

"Of course I do," I said, elated.

"Then give him our regards."

"Kol Yisrael haverim," I shouted sarcastically at them. "All Jews are brethren, friends, colleagues. Their hearts quicken when they meet each other in distant places. Instant contact. Hearts speaking. Souls touching. Or haven't you traveled, so haven't you learned?"

I imagined the attitude of these hardhearted women to the poor Jews of the community, and to their poor relative Piadadé, so that the very sight of them tore him from his place. I felt like shouting "Piadadé" at them, just as I had exclaimed "the four women" to him, and prompted him to flee.

"What have you done for others?" I roared.

"What have you?" they snapped in reply, or was it just my words resounding in the tiny room?

Someone tapped lightly on the window. Roza looked up. The tapping insisted. We could not see who it was; it had suddenly grown dark, cloudy.

"You see," Roza hissed. "They are here already. I not even offitzially open. And you buy even zero. You relative, you hear? Relative mine. I tell politzei you relative."

"Ah, politzei. Politzei," the Harreras repeated.

Roza came around the counter, embraced and

kissed me—her lips were thick and deliciously tart—waiting for the agents of the state to open the door and see her with her loving kin.

"Why is the police here?" I said into Roza's ear. The little shop was thick with musk, perfume, the scent of woman's hair.

"The women lose pitcher," she whispered. "Missing. A blue pitcher. But I say nothing."

I leaned against the counter. My hand went to my pocket. Caught. Trapped. My head swirled. I tried to put together the sequence of events, but like reading before dozing off, the words, the thoughts, danced and bent; they refused to tread a straight line. I watched the door. There was no one knocking. I felt relieved. The Harreras I could handle, but I was afraid of the police.

"But there's no one knocking," I said. I immediately—without even thinking—translated this to Hebrew and noted the double-entendre for the sexual act. Donatello Ferrari, had his spirit come into mine along with Yehuda Halevi's?

Still embracing me, Roza did not remove her eyes from the window.

"But there's no one knocking," I repeated the refrain from lines as yet unwritten.

"You stay," she whispered, "and I no tell them."

"Can't. Not now. I have to pay the man. I'll come back later."

"Hailstones," the Harreras said.

"Does it hail here in the summer?" I asked in disbelief. "The Jewish travel guide said nothing about hail."

"Books omit many things," the eldest sister said. "They conceal more than they reveal. We are in the mountains. Rain turns to hail. Dew falls in Israel. Now let us go. We must go home before the heavy hailstones fall."

I did not move.

Roza returned behind the counter. "Maybe *he* tell you about the pitcher."

All four Harreras, with their sharp noses and thin old wrinkled faces, looked at me.

"You?" they said.

"Perhaps on Tuesday," I said. "At home."

"Now," the eldest said. "Tell us about the pitcher."

"Will you open the museum boxes for me?"

"Yes," they said. "Tell us."

"First the boxes. Let's go to the museum."

Then Roza said something to them in the native language. Their faces tightened. They leaned forward, but I was already at the door, out the door, running in the hail, hand in pocket, protecting the little pitcher that was mine but not yet fully mine because I hadn't paid for it. The white, rice-sized pellets nipped gently. First I had given chase, and now I myself was being chased. I turned around. The four women loped, ran, leaped, agile for their age. Roza, her face was pressed against the glass. Her white nose looked like a button of dough.

I ran ahead, but the four women kept up their pursuit, as after a thief. I saw one of the women brush a drop of water from her eye, regally, like a queen. "What have you?" the sisters challenged me, far behind me now.

The hail was letting up. Now only a few small hailstones fell, like afterthoughts. They did not crack the tiles or penetrate the roofs but themselves were broken into harmless sprinkles of ice. Faint sunlight shone, even as the last of the hailflakes were falling.

Then, as suddenly as it had come, the hail ceased, as though a covenant had been remembered. A shaft of bluish light, lost section of a rainbow, passed swiftly over the sky.

I turned. The women were not in sight. No sounds of pursuit. I stopped, wanted to see my pitcher again. Enclosed, it was not mine. Viewed, it was mine once more. Received anew, like a beloved possession one sees after long absence. I opened the cloth bag—felt a little plosive movement in my chest, heart bursting, then the rush of blood choking me. The pitcher—it was now a crude clay jug.

"Piadadé," I shouted.

"Piadadé!" I cried.

Now *I* wanted to run, give chase, pursue, like the Harreras after their phantasmagoric prey, but I did not know where to go. A large grey cloud covered the sky and the hail began again. It was softer now, more like snow, and it came down slowly, thickly, as though in a dream. I brushed a flake from my eyelid, unconsciously using the sister's slow, regal gesture. I saw geometric stars, six-pointed stars, crenellated Stars of David, hexagons with extended rills, little wheels whose spokes carried tiny hammers. Hail floated as if someone above had just shaken an enormous pillow of cold goose feathers.

The hail, which oddly warmed my face on touch, tapped lightly, swirled all about. I remembered an ice snow like this during my childhood; I was happy that it had turned my cheeks warm and red, cheeks glowing red from warmth and cold. My mother kissed my cheek. Delicious as an apple, she said. But I was not happy now. Now I felt betrayed. The hail was thick.

Street and houses were effaced. I slowly made my way forward. Perhaps around any corner the Harreras were waiting for me. What now? Now I was dead indeed. Finished. The image I had used for Rabbi Gagliata-cozzo came back to haunt me. A man, waiting all his life to go to Israel, arrives, but once his plane lands he's blindfolded and sent back. Why had Piadadé deceived me? Why had he given me the opportunity of outwitting him when all along he was planning to outfox me? For this I could not forgive him. He had stirred up my appetite and then denied it. I looked up. The sky had grown so dark it seemed like dusk. I walked and walked and nothing happened, like in a nightmare.

Then I stood still and felt I was on a raft being slowly propelled forward, deeper and deeper into the labyrinth of the bazaar. I might just as well have been in a deserted field or forest. The hell with it, I thought. Was this what I was destined to find? Hailstones and a cheap clay jug? The four women and their exhibition frustrated me at every turn. Piadadé had deceived me. Yussuf, no help. Even Roza, warm, inviting, seductive, a mind reader, one step ahead of my thoughts, Roza in the store, her olive skin and moist mouth, those serpents writhing alive around her ears, even Roza had betrayed me. I shivered again. What if I were lost? I had seen my name in the Book of the Dead, but seeing it created a paradox. Seeing one's own name in the Book of the Dead means that one is still in the Book of the Living. One of the two possibilities is false: either the seeing or the listing.

But I was in the city. People get lost in forests, in mountains, at sea. They don't get lost in city streets. Yet here I couldn't even tell anyone I was lost. Which meant I was lost indeed. My heart pounded with fear even before I felt the fear; and then I tasted that sour sensation in back of my throat—the taste a trapped animal must feel before it is slain.

I focused on myself. Considered what the four women had shouted at me, cleverly inverting my accusation against them. Throwing back at me the mirror of my indignation. What have *you* done for others?

What, indeed, I thought as I brushed along the wooden structures. I pressed the pitcher to my chest, hoping that when I opened the cloth bag again, I would be surprised. I touched the walls of the wooden buildings, for comfort, not guidance. I was wet and tired, and—yes!—frightened going through that white tunnel. Collecting knowledge and manuscripts and pitchers and coins; whom did all this benefit? Had any of this ever saved one human being from sorrow?

Then through the opaque mist—it felt like a song of triumph; a shift of key signature—I saw a light in a window: I left the security of the rough wood wall and headed for the light.

IV

The Pharmacy

I entered a silent room and shut the door behind me. Terra firma, not white void, a place of light. A chandelier with a dozen thick candles illuminated the room. Candles in brass holders in various wall niches gave added light and made it smell like a church on saints day. Everywhere on the dark wooden shelves stood jars of various sizes. On a counter toward the back I saw a huge elaborate scale. I took a deep breath, exhaled a heavy sigh: suspiration. Fragrances of medicines and herbs, odors of dried grasses, hay and leaves, lemons, berries, and spices.

The pharmacist came in from behind a curtain. Because of the dim light I hardly noticed him in back of the room. He nodded and gestured for me to wait. Without saying a word, he took a brass mortar and pestle and, while gazing at a piece of parchment before him, began mixing ingredients. Another fragrance, sweet and bitter, wafted over the room.

From holding the pitcher so close to my chest, I developed a cramp in my left forearm. I placed the pitcher, wrapped in its cloth bag, on a niche in the wall near the doorway and rubbed my arm.

"A salve for your arm, young man," the pharmacist

said. "It will make your muscle warm. Comfortable. Come, come here."

He lifted his face, which emerged from the shadow. He held up a vial, filled with liquid, to examine it in the light. I walked across the room. At once I was struck— Lord, I was stunned! There I was: oval face, high cheek-bones, rounded chin, clever long green eyes, large head—when I'm photographed from below I give the appearance of being tall and powerful, whereas I have a medium frame, for which the large head compensates: nature always compensates—powerful shoulders and torso, muscular forearms, long delicate aristocratic fingers that never need to be taught to hold the pinkie out while drinking tea. The same sandy brown hair, curly but not kinky. But then I saw that he was older, as though I'd been projected into a time-mirror and had seen myself twenty-five years from now. No one wishes to see oneself suddenly older, just as no one wishes to note his official disappearance or demise in a Book of the Dead.

"Curt," I said instinctively. I felt odd reciting my own name. I had never known anyone else with my name, and had never addressed myself.

The man inclined his head. "The salve? Shall I prepare it for you, my son?"

The door opened and two old women wearing long black dresses and mantillas swept in: the Harreras again. I quickly hid in the shadows in the back. One held the door open for the third, who supported the eldest woman. She walked in slowly, her head trembling, and approached the pharmacist. I felt a twitch in my heart. "What have *you?*" Like a live grenade cast back to the thrower, their question ricocheted back to me and exploded.

The pharmacist bowed. "Shalom," he said, and took a piece of paper from her hand. He looked at it and said, "Shall I send a boy with the medicine?"

"No, I am afraid he will spill it. We shall return for it." The woman picked up an azure blue porcelain pitcher on the pharmacist's counter and examined it.

"What is it, Donna Beracha? Do you see a flaw?"

"No," she said slowly, turning the pitcher. "But curious, it looks like one of ours." The pharmacist smiled politely as she raised it, examined the bottom, and ran her fingers over it. "No, no, it cannot be." Carefully, as though it were a rare dish of her own, she set the blue pitcher back on the counter.

At the door, she whispered to her sisters, "It looked so much like our stolen one my heart sank. Of course, the pharmacist's is totally worthless."

I shivered again. A corkscrew of depression bit into me. Indeed a novice might have taken the pharmacist's pitcher to be similar to the one I had bought from Piadadé, but it was like comparing an oil painting to a reproduction. But even at the expense of gaining the Harreras' favor, perhaps getting them to open their collection, a collection, I realized, that might be totally worthless, I did not want to implicate Piadadé, who— there was no denying it now: all signs pointed to it— had stolen it from them. And perhaps they might even consider me a thief as well, an accomplice who had several times accosted them. And what good would my—a stranger's—word have been in a land where the police was powerful? So there was no bargain to be struck after all. I could only lose my freedom, not gain the chests.

Again I shivered. The warmth had finally settled into me, displacing the cold from the storm outside. I was puzzled. How is it that these women, who had come in after a hailstorm, were perfectly dry; not a snowflake on their mantillas; not a droplet of water on their clothing? And when had they had time to change?

"But it's been hailing outside," I wanted to call as they filed out calmly, heads regally up, old aristocrats on parade. Again the first woman held the door. I looked out. The sunny stillness of a spring day; warm air, dry streets.

Just as the last of the women was shutting the door, a twelve-year-old boy dashed in under her arm with a note in his hand. His small, yellow turban and long, lemon-colored over-shirt gave him a princely look. The pharmacist ran toward him, but did not greet him with "Shalom." He took the paper without a word and went to a cabinet recessed into a wall at the side of the room where obviously the most potent medicines were stored. The pharmacist inserted a key, jiggled it, muttered in disappointment, but could not open the cabinet door. The boy urged him on. My heart began to beat in fear, as though I were the boy who couldn't get his medicine quickly, as though I were the pharmacist who could not open the door. The pharmacist stood the boy on a chair and asked him to insert the key. The boy tried, did not succeed. The pharmacist inserted other keys, then pieces of metal and wood. At first the lad was patient, even cooperative, but now as the wait lengthened and he did not get his medicine, he became abusive, calling out monosyllabic words in a high-pitched voice in a language I could barely understand. I stepped forward and asked the pharmacist for the key. Resignedly, he gave it to me. It was an old-fashioned wooden key, an antique, the like of which I had not seen before. The cabinet door, I noticed, was made out of thick marble. I slipped it into the lock, heard the two notches clicking, but could not turn the key.

The boy kept up his impudent chattering, looking off to the side as though afraid to squarely meet the pharmacist's eye.

"Oh woe," the pharmacist broke his silence. "I must get this medicine closet open. It is for the boy's grandfather, Pladjrude."

"Isn't there a locksmith here?" I asked.

The pharmacist did not reply. He ran out a rear door which opened into a sunny courtyard decorated with rose bushes and lemon trees. He ran across the courtyard and came back with two distinguished-looking elders. To his quick pace they walked measured steps. Dressed in white cloaks and tall, grey, cylindrical hats, they entered the pharmacy and went straight to the medicine cabinet. The pharmacist gave them the key and returned to the counter. The men too attempted to insert and turn the key. I recognized one of the elders as Piadadé, but his eyes were not sad now and there was nothing harried or ill-dressed about him. He looked at me, but not a muscle moved on his face. The second resembled Rabbi Gagliatacozzo; he had the same short, sturdy build, but his mustache was grey, his sideburns white.

"Don't you recognize me?" I asked Piadadé.

The men looked startled, as though wondering why I was addressing them.

"What sort of game are you playing?" I told Piadadé. The men exchanged glances.

"Give me my pitcher! I wanted to pay you. Even three times more than you asked for." Then I faced the rabbi. "Rabbi, I bought a porcelain pitcher from him but he substituted a worthless clay jug." I pointed to the niche in the wall where I had left the pitcher.

Now they began laughing, as if I'd said something absurd, repeating the words "pitcher" and "rabbi," savoring them, rolling them over on their tongues and laughing.

I looked about for the audience. Obviously I'd stumbled onto a stage, and the actors were ignoring me, the intruder into their rite. What sort of masquerade was this? They were so immersed in their local ritual, they did not recognize me. Yet there was no stage, no audience that I could see. Or was it that the Jews in this small town had intermarried among themselves so long they began to resemble one another?

"What shall we do?" said the man who resembled Rabbi Gagliatacozzo. "It will surely cause trouble with the regime. They will say that Jews refused to cure him. A Jewish plot, they will say."

Piadadé nodded gravely.

"Well, aren't you going to say something?" I said. "Or is there no justice here even among the Jews? *Kol Yisrael haverim* is Greek to you."

Just then a door from the other side was pushed open. The candles flickered with the shock of air. I picked up my pitcher from the niche. When I lifted it from its protective cloth bag, no miracle: red loam baked clay jug, they were sold three for a porud in the bazaar. I looked at the red clay and imagined my porcelain pitcher, its vivid colors, blue and green, yellow and rose, and the pharmacy painted on it. I remembered the medicine cabinet between the vined rills and the intertwining rosebuds, as if I saw them now. I turned the pitcher in my mind to find the script on the pitcher, but could not recall it: I had only seen the shape of the letters, not the words.

Meanwhile, more people entered, but the room turned not darker but bright, as though each man had brought his own candle with him. Murmuring and shouts. The pharmacy had become a marketplace. A huge, perspiring man, a butcher, judging by the apron he wore, was twisting a heavy piece of wood into the lock. He fiercely jabbed in the wood, then threw up his hands.

Through the rear doorway, across the courtyard, I saw a tavern. A redheaded boy ran in, made his way between two men merrily doing a jig. He approached a third man, who sat with his face down on the table, his right hand clasping a bowl of beer. "Menlos," he said, tapping the man's shoulder and pulling his ear. "Menlos!" he shouted. The tavern keeper came and sprinkled water on Menlos's face and helped him up. Menlos shook himself, and wiped his face. The other man whispered into Menlos's ear. The look of merriment faded; it struggled, however, with the lingering cheerful mien.

Menlos stood and, with surprising agility for an inebriated man, strode forward confidently. Followed by the redhead, Menlos crossed the courtyard, plucked a lemon from the lemon tree, bit off the top and sucked on the flesh without so much as changing the expression on his face. People made way for Menlos as if he were a boat coming through—"Menlos, Menlos," they susurrated—like waves they gathered to the left and right and prepared an opening for the prow of his stride.

"Right here," Menlos shouted. "We don't need nowhere else. Right here we'll hold court. Where's the pharmacist?"

"Here, your honor," someone called.

"Silence," he boomed. He pulled a hammer from his pocket and banged the table. At that moment, he looked like Yussuf banging shut on me the lid to the box I'd never gotten to see.

I now saw the judge's face. The shamash, Dom Domingo, I whispered to myself. The face is the face of Dom Domingo, but the hand is the hand of Yussuf. But why were they calling him Menlos? What was happening here? Perhaps a city pageant? No part was given to me; yet I too spoke and was spoken to. So what, then, was my role here? And why did the pharmacist resemble me so closely? A resemblance so pointed it disoriented me. There was no doubt the pharmacist looked like me. It takes oneself to know oneself.

Menlos, so recently drunk, sat at the table playing the judge. He called the pharmacist, looked about, then snapped his fingers. The redhead who had awakened him came to him; Menlos pointed to the scale on the pharmacist's counter. A moment later the scale was set up at the judge's table. The weights moved back and forth, but Menlos stilled them until they balanced perfectly. With a wave of his hand silence came over the room.

"Your name?" he asked the pharmacist.

There was a moment of hesitation. I felt the weight of silence on me, a palpable pressure, like that caused by the peaks over Mustara, until I almost said: Curt Leviant, for I knew the words were addressed to me.

Meanwhile, the pharmacist had already said his name, and I had not heard.

"Now tell me your name," the judge asked the turbaned lad.

"Mjerl," he said, and then added proudly, "I am the grandson of Pladjrude, who now lies ill."

"What is your complaint?"

The boy said that the pharmacist had not given him the prescribed medicine; not only had he not given it, but he had abused the lad for insisting upon it.

"Refusing medicines to an ill man is a capital offence according to the law," Judge Menlos said.

"I have never refused anyone medicines," the pharmacist said in a firm voice. "There are many here in this room who have received medicines from me." The pharmacist looked at the crowd. "Slavko? You. Tell the judge how I saved your life. Or you, Semja? Ibrahin. Pedro. Zoja. Cardinale. Stjoki."

As he called their names, they looked away, turned their heads aside one after another like mechanical dolls.

"Of course he never refused them medicines. He never refused me either!" Piadadé said.

But you deceived me. You stole a pitcher, I almost shouted. Menlos! Try Piadadé, the thief.

"On the contrary," Piadadé continued. "He often gives medications without charge to the poor who cannot pay."

"Of course. To Jews," the judge said. "Why not? Jews always love Jews—but hate the rest. So it is written in your holy books."

"Not so," the pharmacist called. "Love your fellow man as yourself is meant for everyone."

"Be still," Menlos said. "*You* are on trial here. Not the books. Don't try to change the subject. Why didn't you want to give the boy the medicine?"

"I wanted to. But I cannot open the medicine chest."

"Why is it locked?" asked the judge.

"By law, potent medicines have to be locked . . . And the lock is broken. This has never happened before."

"Witchcraft! Magic!" came a voice from the crowd. "Powders. Potions. Like his medicines."

The turn of the conversation frightened me. My heart pounded. I took a deep breath. The unique pharmacy scent was now gone. The crowd had replaced it with a thick aroma of its own. The candles and the many men pressed together brought out a smell of wax and sweat.

"Your honor," the pharmacist said. "Here is the key. It will not work. See for yourself."

The judge laughed. "No intelligent man will believe that. We're not boors! We don't believe in demons or magic or witchcraft. This is obviously a plot of the Jews. I know your intrigues. If Pladjrude dies, there will be a struggle for power and the Jews will support— Oh, I know your intrigues."

"On the contrary, we like Pladjrude very much," the pharmacist countered, "and I myself am very fond of him."

"All the more reason to wonder why you are plotting his death. Leave it to the Jews."

Menlos then made a churning motion with his hands, as though cranking up a wheel.

"The Jews! The Jews!" the crowd responded.

Pladjrude's grandson stepped up to the judge's table. "And you know what? The pharmacist told me he couldn't care less if Grandfather died or not, and that is why he is not giving me any medicine."

"That is right," voices echoed. "We heard it."

"Not so," said the pharmacist. "Pladjrude trusts me.

That's why he sent his grandson, Mjerl, to get medicines I prepare . . . What the boy is saying is not so."

"The boy is lying," I added. I *think* I added.

I closed my eyes for a moment. The disorientation was complete. I felt removed from myself, perched on an observer's platform watching myself as in a dream. I dreamt I was away from home, in a new land, ready to serve my people in an hour of need like the legendary medieval Jewish knight.

"The boy is lying," I said. "The pharmacist did not say that. He could not open the lock. I too tried and failed."

"He could not open the lock," Piadadé said.

"*We* could not open it," Rabbi Gagliatacozzo added.

The butcher stepped forward, wiping his hands on his red-stained apron.

"I could not open the lock," he roared.

"None of us could open the lock," the Jews said.

"You," Menlos pointed to me. "Yes, you. Who are you?"

"What do you mean? I am myself."

"Don't give us riddles. You spoke up before. Speak now. Tell the court your name."

"Curt Leviant."

Again Menlos snapped his fingers. A young woman brought in a register of names. I looked at her—the shopkeeper's attractive wife. So Roza too had a part in the proceedings. Her I could convince, intrigue, seduce. I walked up to Roza and took her hand. Indignant, she withdrew, as though touched by hot coal.

Menlos opened the book, ran his finger down a list of names.

"You're not here. There is no Curt Leviant."

"There is," I shouted. "Even she knows me."

The judge poked her with his elbow. "Go take a look at him. Do you know him?"

Roza looked at me. Of course it was her—the same oval olive face, burning ember eyes, and well-fleshed lips. The same breasts that not long ago had pressed into my arms. Roza shrugged.

"Go to the Jewish Museum," I said. "See the Memorial Book. Of course I'm there. I'm on the list, between Levia and Leviatan."

Menlos snickered. "What Jewish Museum? Have the Jews built a museum here? What book? The man is singing tales from the *Arabian Nights.*"

He burst out laughing and everyone laughed raucously with him.

Menlos banged the table. Though he did not appear to be drunk, his face was flushed and his eyes red and starting from their sockets.

"The court has decided that for your refusal to cure an ill man—"

"I did not refuse," the pharmacist said. "I could not open—Try it yourself."

Menlos played with the scale, watching the sides rock back and forth.

"According to the law, refusal to administer medicines is punishable by—"

The assembled crowd in the pharmacy caught its breath. I breathed deeply too and inhaled the smell of the hostile crowd instead of medicinal fragrances.

"*I* won't say it," Menlos said. "Let the people speak. Open the doors. All of them. Front and back. To the courtyard and to the shops."

The doors were opened. Sunlight flooded in from all directions. The smells of lemons and roses wafted in, mingling with the scents of crowd and cumin and sassafras. From everyone, from the garden, from the youths on the lemon trees trying to get a better view, from the tavern, from the shops, from the crowd gathered outside by the front door, from those around the table and in the pharmacy came the chorus, the united cry, the voice of the people:

"Death to the Jews!"

The pharmacist's head fell. When it rose, he looked straight at me. A shiver rilled through my body. He recognized me—himself—his alter ego in the Jewish passion play.

Menlos banged on the table with the hammer, tipped the brass scale. "The people have spoken. But since we are not cruel, not bloodthirsty, you may choose your own manner of death, as prescribed in your own holy prayers: hanging, beheading, burning, or drowning."

What was I to do now? No script, no prompter to coach me. No rehearsal. No precedent. I walked up to the pharmacist and put my hand on his.

"*Kol Yisrael haverim,*" he said. "Except Menlos."

"What do you mean?"

"His mother was Jewish. He is one of ours. The worst kind."

"Drowning," I said.

"What?"

"Drowning. Choose drowning."

Because I hoped the film would split, break, get wet; because the pages his story was being written on would get soggy and the ink would run, the letters would be washed away, the edge of the judgment dissolved, and his life would be saved. Or perhaps if fire— the curtain would come down to save the audience and let the hero escape in time. But the truth is—I don't know why I said drowning.

"Why drowning?" the pharmacist asked.

But just then the question sparked the answer, and I replied: "Because God promised Noah he would not again destroy the world by drowning, and doesn't the Talmud teach us that he who kills one man is seen as one who kills an entire world, and hence by killing you with drowning it is as though God would be destroying an entire world contrary to His promise and His law— choose death by drowning and you won't die."

"Drowning," the pharmacist said aloud in a clear firm voice.

"But," Menlos lifted a finger: at that moment he looked just like Dom Domingo pointing at the plush chairs in the beautiful hidden synagogue. "But since we are compassionate too we will not execute judgment at once, but permit you to rectify your wrong. We will fill one of your medical basins partly with water. If you tell us how to open the cabinet, you will be spared. If not, we will keep adding water until you drown."

Menlos's long wooden table was bare. An assistant brought a wide porcelain basin and poured some water into it. Menlos tilted the pharmacist's head back into the basin.

"More water," Menlos ordered.

The assistant poured. Then the judge stayed his hand and took the pitcher in his hand, admiring it.

Dom Domingo, I wanted to shout.

"Well, will you tell us how to open the cabinet?"

"I cannot open it," the pharmacist said. "No one can. There is nothing to add."

"Except water," said Menlos. "Pour more."

Now the water was up to his forehead and over his ears. Then it covered his eyes, the bridge of his nose. No one held the pharmacist's head; with perfect self-control, with perfect faith, he did not lift his head. Soon the pharmacist would drown, contrary to my promise. I felt ashamed in the bright warm spotlight, What have *you*? the Harreras asked me.

At this point I looked at that worthless jug again, but saw again the pitcher I should have had. I remembered the little pitcher which showed a man with his head in a basin, the water just up to his mouth. If we were reliving history, if there was truth to Piadadé's statement: "Perhaps it can open up doors" (and perhaps a thief could be a liar too), then I *had* to move now. Forward with the pitcher, the cloth bag cast aside—the clay jug was not really ugly; despite its darkness it had a certain linear grace—toward the judge, as though in a dream. As though I myself were participating in a rite whose significance I did not know but under whose spell I was. Dom Domingo, I recalled, loved beautiful objects. A neat concatenation of events. Which again pointed to me.

A thick, musty silence in the room. Two sides of a chorus looked at me. The Harreras spoke to me. I let them. I accepted their words. What had I done indeed? The water was rising on the pharmacist's head and I was moving toward him with the red clay jug in my hand and the Harrera sisters were coming through the door for their medicine, watching me holding the clay jug that Piadadé had slyly substituted for the real one, moving swiftly now, that eagle sharp look on their faces—"There! There it is!"

I decided to present the jug to Menlos and tell him it was a rare old pitcher. But then came the moment that pained me most. I hesitated. Thinking: Perhaps Piadadé considered it worthless, whereas in truth it really *was* a precious antique. I hesitated. Just a fraction of a second. I was ashamed. The pharmacist's eye caught mine. He looked at me upside down, through the water, but he saw me nevertheless. I began to sweat. My face, my neck were soaking wet. "There it is," the Harreras hissed, coming closer. The water slowly rose. It flowed into my ears, making lapping sounds, like waves slapping against a moored boat.

On the ceiling, or perhaps he stood over me, I saw the Jeremiah eyes of Piadadé who had stolen a pitcher. I regretted wanting to take the pitcher from him; I should have given him the money as a gift, done as I used to do in the subways when I threw a dime into a blind pencil seller's cap and never took a pencil. What good was scholarship without kindness? On the other hand, why should I repay kindness for malice? Piadadé had fooled me. Why should I feel sympathy toward him? If I missed my chance now with the Harreras, when I held the trump card in my hand, I'd lose my chance forever. I'd tell the women about their rascal cousin and they'd let me see their treasure.

The water rose above my face. I gasped for breath. What had gone wrong? What had I done? What should I have done? The dream had gone out of control. Why was I being drowned? Because so it was written, so it was pictured, so it was destined—and I was merely witness like to a motion picture which one can see again

152

and again and predict the course of events, but can neither change its outcome nor alter the fate of the players.

So this was the way I died. The previous Rosh Hashana I had chanted: who shall live and who shall die, who by fire, who by water, who by famine, who by plague? So my death, then, was water, and that was why my name was inscribed in neat black letters on that textured, off-white, thick paper with flaking lint in the large red book that hangs—yes hangs—in the Jewish Museum, as though it itself were victim. But by seeing my name in that Book of the Dead, I created a paradox. And creation is a sign—co-equal, result—of life. And there was another paradox: if I did not exist, if my name did not appear on any list, I could not be judged, could not be drowned. So though the water was up to my nostrils, my hair wet, my forehead, my ears, my temples immersed, the bridge of my nose under water, but my nostrils still free, I was still still still master of my fate.

"One moment," I said.

"You have something to tell us?" Menlos said.

"Yes, this antique pitcher in my hand."

I assumed many things. That I would take the pitcher to the medicine cabinet and with the force of Piadadé's promise, "Perhaps it can open up doors" (but it did already: it opened up apartment doors for him), have it serve as an incantation. Place it to the door and it would, as in a dream, open the lock. Provide the magic that Menlos rejected. Or perhaps from the spout of the pitcher I could anoint the lock with magic oil and open the door. I had not gone this far to be turned back now.

My fantasy was broken by the stunning silence. I lifted my head from the water. The water ran down my neck into my back. No one prevented me from standing—a good omen. At this point, the man who was playing Piadadé raised his hand in a fist, and taking advantage of the silence, opened his hand and said, "This new gold coin to the first who can open the lock."

Two men standing outside by the lemon tree in the courtyard raced to the cabinet.

The pitcher was placed on the table. Now so many things happened I cannot recall the order of events. The four-headed hawk with one soul, one thrust, one determination, was upon me. "We found it," the women said triumphantly.

Some in the crowd shouted encouragement to the two men picking the lock in the marble doors recessed into the wall.

Menlos examined the pitcher.

Piadadé bent forward to hold it.

Roza surged forward to seize it herself.

The four Harreras leaped with united breath and will to the pitcher. "The heirloom!"

Hands outstretched.

Where was I? I don't know where I was. By the wall, near the niche in the back of the pharmacy? Or near the table and viewing events through the far side of a telescope? And where was the pharmacist? Up from the water?

But all this does not matter, for none of the hands that went for the pitcher grasped that pitcher, for in the tangle of hands, the clash of wills, the Harreras knocked that pitcher and the hammer from the table.

The judge jumped forward. And this time I was not there—though again I saw it in slow motion sailing to the floor—to save it. Like a drop of water at the moment of impact, I saw the pitcher cleave and break in two as hammer and floor struck it. But what was that that fell with a dull clang to the ground? Out of the pitcher? Built into it to be released at moment of impact? The dying of one yielding the birth of another? Out of the mouth of the precious (or worthless) comes the sweet? From the broken vessel the key to salvation. So the Harreras and I were destined after all to meet, converge, in point of time and deed. I bent down and quickly picked up the key and thrust, pushed, shoved, no politeness now, elbowed my way through the crowd to the marble cabinet door, inserted the key, gave one twist, heard the neat click and opened the lock, opened the door.

"Our pitcher, our heirloom," the Harrera sisters cried.

"The key was found because of you!" Menlos shouted. "Our thanks to you!"

A shout of joy came from the crowd. The pharmacist, his hair dripping, pressed my shoulders but said nothing. I was glad. I did not want him to say anything. He removed the medicine and went to his counter, preparing it for Mjerl's grandfather and for the Harreras.

Piadadé pressed the coin into my hand.

"No," I said. "It was their pitcher. Give it to them."

I was curious to see the Harreras' reaction when Piadadé would approach them. They did not avert their eyes or snub him. They took the large gold coin and even seemed pleased. The eldest sister, her head trembling, held the two neatly broken halves of the pitcher as if considering how it could be mended. They looked right through me, as if I weren't there.

As the pharmacist prepared the medicine, he poured a liquid from a jar and then added new ingredients, mixing with mortar and pestle. He poured the mixture into a flask and gave it to Mjerl. Then he beckoned to me. From the counter he picked up the sky-blue porcelain pitcher that the Harreras had examined earlier. He dipped a quill into blue ink and carefully began to write, filling the blank side of the pitcher with tiny lines of Hebrew verse, lines that I already knew before he wrote them, and decorating it with blue irises and green-stemmed roses intertwined in a Shah Abbas Persian carpet design. Then he added sunflowers and lemons, scenes from the trial and pictures of his pharmacist shop. When he finished, he said, "Here, my son," and presented me the pitcher with a silent look of gratitude. The smile he gave me was perhaps like the one that God gave Moses at the burning bush. One of the sparks from that fire was in the pharmacist's eyes as he looked at me.

By now the crowd had dispersed through the rear doors into the courtyard—the tavern I could see was busier and nosier than before—and the pharmacy was filled again with its former fragrances and scents.

Outside the sun was shining. Pitcher in hand, I walked in the sunshine. The snow had melted, the hail was gone. A fine clean smell of air, lambent air after a rain or after a snowfall, the tangy inspiration of air after weeping. I walked the streets, wound through the lanes of the deserted bazaar, wound my steps like tefillin straps around its alleyways, until I reached the square of the white pigeons. The famous white pigeons of Mustara, which lies high in the mountains, halfway between the oppressive snowcaps and the azure sea.

Library of American Fiction

Melvin Jules Bukiet
Stories of an Imaginary Childhood

Rebecca Goldstein
Mazel

Curt Leviant
Ladies and Gentlemen, the Original Music of the Hebrew Alphabet
and *Weekend in Mustara*

About the Author

Curt Leviant is the author of five critically acclaimed novels, *The Yemenite Girl, Passion in the Desert, The Man Who Thought He Was Messiah, Partita in Venice,* and *Diary of an Adulterous Woman.* He has won the Edward Lewis Wallant Award and writing fellowships from the National Endowment for the Arts, the Rockefeller Foundation, the Jerusalem Foundation, and the New Jersey Arts Council. His short stories and novellas have appeared in *Midstream, Zoetrope, American Literary Review, Confrontation, North American Review, Missouri Review, Ascent, Tikkun,* and many other magazines, and on National Public Radio. His work has been included in *Best American Short Stories, Prize Stories: The O. Henry Awards,* and other anthologies. Mr. Leviant's first novel, *The Yemenite Girl,* has been translated into Hebrew and Spanish.